WAGGING TALES
VOLUME 1

The First Offering

and other stories

Vijay Padaki

INDIA • SINGAPORE • MALAYSIA

For

Chatura

Vijay's stories don't so much transport me to another world as take me to other planes of this one. They are a hall of mirrors where each reflection gives us a glimpse of the extraordinary in what seems at first to be a mundane life. His tales never fail to remind me that everyone is unique, complex, born from miraculous histories, carriers of the oldest tragedies and most ancient mythologies, without even realizing it.

Jeffrey Stanley
Fulbright Ambassador, Playwright,
Professor of Stage and Film writing, Drexel University and Tisch School

Vijay Padaki's stories are arresting for his range of subjects, not restricted by class, religion or ethnicity. They are those of an observer who has had a multitude of experiences but who has kept a wry distance from the human situations that have excited his imagination. Although he has evident sympathies he does not take sides or judge, and his concise prose delivers each tale with an impact that should be the envy of most Indian fiction writers in English today."

MK Raghavendra
Cultural, Film and Literary critic and Writer

Vijay's stories, like his plays, have a cinematic quality to them. The imagery makes available lasting images that forge their way through profound and deceptive simplicity of woven words. The punch moves subtly, almost imperceptibly, through the fabric of language to make for the unexpected twist at the end, time and again, as always.

Padmavati Rao
Actor, Poet, Storyteller, Educator

These short stories will bring you the old world fragrance of fresh coffee in a tumbler and firewood in the old bath house. Vijay Padaki melds his background in psychology, theatre and management to bring alive characters, relationships, dynamics and interactions in unique settings. The detailing and denouement in each story is exquisite.

Shekhar Seshadri
Child & Adolescent Psychiatrist,
Theatre Educator, Musician

ISBN 979-8-89588-658-8

CONTENTS

Telling Stories

A few ideas have stayed with me over many years. The first is that when the human animal discovered the advantages of living and moving in groups, rather than as loner hunter-gatherers, the first joy was in the new experience of sharing – sharing food from the hunt, sharing experiences from the hunt, sharing learnings, sharing ideas...sharing stories. The craft of storytelling was recognized for its value as early as the craft of making spears or skinning animals.

The second idea is something I picked up from an old British playwright friend who, unfortunately, is no more. It was a most remarkable idea. He said that mankind has only six stories. The six stories are based on a small number of primal experiences for which the human species has an innate capacity. All the stories ever told by mankind are really combinations of these primal experiences. The combinations can be infinite, of course. Not very different from the infinite range of hues that a paint company can turn out for us – all from three basic colours. The same as the three concentrates in your colour printer.

The third is that all writing is autobiographical. The qualifier would be: to greater or lesser extent. What that means is that life experiences have a way of creeping into everything we say. In other words, there is no need to deny it or be sorry about it. I have had the good fortune of exposures in life that had both breadth and depth. These included field experiences as part of work in large development programmes in rural settings. There is also the curse of indelible memory one has learned to live with. Ah, that is a story in itself. Not surprisingly, many of my stories (not all) are 'case studies', but retold in fictional form.

The fourth is a human characteristic that is usually not given sufficient attention. It is undoubtedly the most fascinating characteristic of the human animal. Among all the 8.7 million species of life on this earth, it is only the human animal that inflicts its experiences on fellow humans. It is the only species that has storytellers. And invents infinite varieties of construction to tell the same six stories.

So...Here I am, trying to hold your attention with a bunch of stories that I have the audacity to believe are original! Here is a paragraph I wrote once to serve as an over-riding preface to every story in my collection of plays for the stage and, now, short stories for reading.

> *I shall cut a long story short. It is a tale that is very old, as old as mankind itself. It has been engraved on stone tablets, inscribed on palm leaves, inked by hand on stretches of hand-made papyrus and passed on in oral storytelling traditions wherever communities gathered to assert their belongingness. It is a tale that can be told through the night or printed on hundreds of pages. I have chosen to tell you the tale in ten minutes. Don't go away if you are listening to me. Don't put the pages down if you are reading. Surely you can spare ten minutes to know what I wish to share with you.*

A final thought. I have had the good fortune to be invited to read my stories to small invited audiences. I discovered first hand then what wise writers have known all along – that the heard text can give us new meanings that the read text does not. I soon found myself writing stories for reading out. It came easily, I suppose, because of the past writing for the stage. The readings have often helped me refine the text. I would like to imagine the stories in this collection having many more readings, even rendered as storytelling theatre.

Many thanks to the close circle that endured the first drafts of these stories. Their comments were always valuable. The circle included Vijji Chari, Madhu Shukla, Priya Rao, Minti Jain, Naveen Tater, Murtuza Khetty, Malavika Kapur and Sudhir and Asha Vombatkere. A second group, comprising the family circle of Chatura, Shabari, Rupande and Shiv, were conscripted into detention for some first readings. More recently Kumkum Amin, taking to writing herself, commented on a few stories. Padmavati (Pinty) Rao and I have done readings together. She convinced me ever so gently that the stories should be published.

I could think of nobody else but Deepak Mote to take charge of the formidable tasks of design, layout and supervision of the publication process.

Vijay Padaki

The Anklet

It was noticed, it was odd, but Malati went about her morning chores trying not to think about it. It was past nine and Devi, the maid, was still in the kitchen. She was drying the dishes with uncommon meticulousness and putting them on the rack on the wall. She had not done that the past two years. It was part of her job, of course, but Malati had stopped asking her to do that ever since Devi had complained about the work load.

"What, Amma! The work in this household is increasing month after month, but there is no change in my pay packet."

"But you are supposed to..."

"How can I manage with what you give me? I have to work in two more places after this house, and one other place twice a week before coming here."

"All I am asking is that you do what you are supposed to do."

"As if you can't dry the vessels and put them on the rack yourself. It's hardly any work. If I get late reaching the next house, they will get really mad."

"And if you run away early from this house I am not supposed to get mad?"

"Ayyo, you can never get mad Amma! Bye Amma!"

That was it. The topic never came up again. The revised schedule was set. Fait accompli they call it. At exactly five minutes before nine there would be a marked speeding up in her movement. In fast forward mode she would dump all the vessels into the large stainless steel basket, toss the napkin into the laundry basket, push the waste basket into its corner with her foot and rush out the second door with a half cheery

"Bye Amma!" Malatiamma would look up at the wall clock. Five to nine.

And here she was on this Monday morning drying dishes and placing them on the rack at nine in the morning. Malati was trying to look busy herself, trying not to notice, trying not to think about it. Maybe the second house had fired her. Maybe they had gone out of town. Maybe she was going to bring up the topic of a raise. A loan. That's it, a loan. No, Malati would not be the first to speak. She would carry on with her work as if nothing had happened. From the puja room she could see that Devi was also carrying on as if nothing had happened. Two women in two rooms of the same house, blissfully immersed in carrying on their morning routines as if it was just another day. After changing the flower decoration in the puja room six times Malati decided to step out and assess the situation. She would not be the first to speak. Just size up the situation.

Devi was at the service door, but did not appear to be leaving. She was leaning against the wall, relaxed. In her hand was something only partly revealed. It looked golden. Without realizing it, Malati spoke first.

"Yes?" There was no response. "You are still here? Aren't you getting late for...?"

First there was a faint smile. Then Devi opened her palm, very slowly, revealing a giant sized anklet of exquisite design. It was old, and it was gold. Malati heard herself gasping. Devi noticed. Malati regretted immediately that she had revealed something – exactly what, she did not know. Never, never reveal your thoughts to servants, her mother-in-law had tutored her when she was inducted into this household as a young bride. Her mind was racing now. This was like nothing Devi had done in her eleven years of service. What on earth was she up to?

"You like it?"

Oh god, she has stolen it! Those people in the eleven o'clock house are rich folks.

"Solid gold, Amma. Twenty-two grade."

How does she know what is solid gold? And how it is graded?

"Tell me, do you like it?"

She is persisting... Where is this heading?

"You are thinking – where is this heading? I will tell you, Amma. What can I hide from you? But first tell me, do you like it?"

Oh god, it is beautiful! But what do I say to her?

"You think it is beautiful?"

"I think it is..."

"It is, isn't it? You will not find one like it in any jewelry shop in this city."

"Why are you showing this to me? Now? Today? Why are you still here?"

"I will tell you Amma."

⌘ ⌘ ⌘ ⌘ ⌘

Malati had to consult Damodar about this. He was a middle ranking officer in a bank. He would know more about such things. They called him Appa all over the neighbourhood, from the milk booth to the barber shop. He liked that. There was a sense of seniority he enjoyed in the neighbourhood that he did not get in the bank.

The evening routine was executed with the same precision as the change of guards at Wagah Border. Damodar would stamp both his feet after the last step on the staircase. This would be followed by three pips of the doorbell before opening it with his own key, as if to alert Amma that she should cover up whatever had been uncovered during his absence. The door would be closed with the left elbow with the briefcase held below while the right hand loosened the tie around the neck. Shoes on the rack, socks spread on top, brief case on the dining table, the tie on the dining chair, and he would exit upstage towards the bathroom with a loud, protracted "Abbabbabbabbaah". Thirty seconds after the sound of the flush he would emerge in a lungi and vest and head for the balcony overlooking the street.

Malati kept a bottle of chilled beer and a bowl of bajjis before Appa, stretched out on the deck chair in the balcony. It was the curtain raiser. She let him be as she busied herself with his favourite dinner of lime rasam and hot chapatis with French beans. She threw in a bowl of gulab jamun at the end. The family physician need never know. Malati suggested that he relax before the TV as she cleared up. She had something to discuss with him. When she reached the bedroom the scene was truly well set for her task. The TV was on, the sound muted, and Appa was dozing before it with a copy of Business Today on his lap. Perfect, she thought. This is how the hypnotists work. Catch them half asleep.

Malati repeated Devi's story to Appa as faithfully as she could.

Devi had run away from the small mofussil town with her aunt when she was thirteen. She had come of age and it was clear what her life was going to be thereafter. The preparations for her grooming had already begun, decreed by caste and community. Her mother was expected to take the lead, as her own mother had twenty years earlier with her. Devi had an aunt who did not agree, and dreamt of another life for her. She made Devi's mother agree to a pact. The pair of gold anklets that she had would be Devi's. It would provide her a secure future. But they would be Devi's only if the mother agreed to her leaving the rural community and going away with the aunt.

It was a long story, not without complications. Malati stopped to check if Appa was with her.

"You follow, no?"

"There is no such thing as a free lunch."

Malati was quite used to conversations with Appa that dipped into his treasure chest of aphorisms. She continued.

"You will ask, how did the aunt get the anklets?"

"You win some, you lose some."

"The aunt had realized long ago that she must have a long term plan."

"In the long term all of us will be dead."

"She would extract the right price from the temple priest for the services rendered."

"Ask not what the country can give you. Ask instead what you can give the country."

And with that his head went limp on the back rest and the magazine dropped off his lap. The mouth was half open, signaling the onset of the first snores. A firm believer in sama veda incantation techniques, Malati decided to implant some more basic information into Appa's sub-conscious in the next few minutes before the deep sleep kicked in. She would then have a productive discussion next morning at breakfast.

Next morning, the aroma of steaming idlis wafting in from the kitchen had the desired effect of awakening Appa's subconscious to elevated levels of comprehension. He opened the conversation with a sharp and crisp observation.

"At the end of the day it all depends on the evaluation of the anklet."

Malati was pleased. He wanted to talk about it. It was in order to respond promptly.

"Two of them."

"She has two anklets?"

"They come in pairs, you know."

"Hmmm. She should not reveal it to anybody else – that she has two of them."

"Nobody else knows she has even one."

"What does she want the money for?"

"What do you think?"

"Not some wedding splurge, I hope. That anklet may be worth lakhs, the way you describe it. Silly how these people waste money on weddings."

"Only business tycoons can do that. Naah, she is not so dumb."

"By the way, two anklets will fetch more than the double of one anklet."

Of course Malati knew that. She was just testing the breeze. And she saw that it was carrying well. The windmill had started to turn. The first step was to get Damodar interested enough. He had to ask for more information, ask for hard data. Only then would he consider some action. He was getting there.

"By the way, there is a premium on gold ornaments crafted before 1960. Also some conditions for their sale. We need to find out how old the anklet is."

Malati could take a stab at that. Devi's aunt got the anklets from the temple priest. The priest got them from the landlord, who claimed his great grandfather had donated jewelry to the deity installed in the temple. The anklet design was unusual, not seen at the jewelers in Malati's lifetime, sparse in detail, exquisite in form and mass. It could be what her mother called turn-of-century design. They were not made to be worn. They were made for display and veneration. You needed sturdy ankles to walk with them. What intoxicant was it that made the landlord pick up the anklets from the family jewel box and given them away to Devi's aunt? He must have been impressed with her ankles.

Neither the description of the anklet nor the story of Devi's spirited aunt interested Appa Damodar. He had to see the anklets himself. He would then decide on a reliable valuation. By the time the second round of idlis arrived he had decided that he should meet Devi personally. Not a word to anybody about this. Just before he picked up the brief case he repeated: Not a word to anybody about this. He stared long into Malati's eyes and then confessed that he was worried. Malati understood. The temple priest and all, there might be complications. It was not that at all, Damodar explained. It was just some unease.

"Uneasy about what?"

"I don't know. It is too much like a bad omen."

"A bad omen?"

"A single anklet, old and rare, large and heavy, priceless, owned by a stranger woman… offered for sale in need... it is so like the story of Kannagi."

"You mean...?"

"And you know how the story ends...death and destruction."

"Aah, but you know what Devi needs the money for?"

"What else? Tell me more in the evening."

He was off. "Tell her about seeing me on Saturday" he reminded her from the top of the staircase. Malati closed the door and sat down for her own breakfast. She had fallen short of her target. Damodar still did not know what Devi wanted to do with the anklet. It had to wait till the evening meal. Anyway, she had got him interested. The idlis in the casserole were still steaming fresh. The sound of Devi's voice in her ear was as fresh, clear as a bell, her words as clear in purpose.

⌘ ⌘ ⌘ ⌘ ⌘

"So there is no 9 o'clock house?"

"No, Amma! But the 11 o'clock house, yes, that one is really there, at the corner of 8th Cross and 4th Main. I go there for one hour and then get back to the 9 o'clock house. I am there till lunch time."

"The 9 o'clock house that is really the 9 o'clock office..."

"It is actually a house, Amma. It is a two-storeyed house made into an office. I was not telling you a lie."

"And you do dusting and cleaning and mopping there, just as in the other houses."

"And making tea at 10 o'clock. I don't do the cleaning-mopping anymore. I just dust the tables and arrange all the papers and files. Then I start on my own work, first entering all the numbers into the computer and attending calls after ten."

It was a chit funds office. They needed people for data entry. There was a lot of work, but the office simply couldn't find people for the job. Devi first showed curiosity about the computer, then an interest in punching keys, and then displayed a flair for data entry that had both speed and accuracy. The office doubled her pay and she was on. At ten, after making the tea, she shifted to the receptionist's desk, took calls, but also continued with her data entry. Above the keyboard she stood up a picture of goddess Meenakshi the size of a playing card. After two years of answering queries on the phone Devi was ready to move on. She had a dream. And she had a plan.

"It will be my own office, Amma. I have found three girls who will work with me. They are good girls, all from our town. When the work is well settled I will double the number. Afterwards, who knows..."

"And the anklet..."

"Like a deposit. I am sure it will fetch enough to take care of at least the first six months – rent, telephone lines, all the computer things we have to buy, paying the girls, and all that. This anklet is very special, no?"

"Somehow the thought of this anklet being sold makes me..."

"No sale, Amma! Never! It will always belong only to me. Some day it will belong to our daughter."

Malati felt relieved. Not without a bit of regret. Somewhere at the back of her mind was the idea that Devi might be offering the anklet for sale to her. She continued, impressed with Devi's business sense.

"Who else knows about this?"

"Nobody. Only you. If my darling aunt was alive I would have talked to her."

"What about your husband?"

"He will get a job in my office."

"No, I mean does he know?"

"Of course not! Not yet. He will know later. Not all the details, but he will know."

There was one other thing Malati had to know. Why her? Why couldn't Devi get the anklet valued by herself and arrange for a gold-loan? A long smile, and Devi replied with another question. Would she ever be able to get the same valuation as Amma's? If Appa can help will it not be even better?

ꕥ ꕥ ꕥ ꕥ ꕥ

Malati prepared for Part Two of the plan. No beer today, she decided. She had to keep Damodar awake. As the footsteps on the staircase approached she ran through the checklist in her mind once more. She was ready. She watched the prologue from the kitchen. "Abbabbabbabbaah". He emerged in his lungi and vest. Seeing the stainless steel tumbler of hot rasam on the living room coffee table he sat down there immediately. Malati joined him with a cup of rasam for herself. She asked if they could continue with the story of Devi.

"Devi an entrepreneur!" Malati had made sure the chat would be in the living room and not on the balcony. She had drawn the curtains and closed the sliding door to the balcony. She had to hush Damodar and ask him to keep his voice low. "Devi an entrepreneur..." he exclaimed again, a little softer. She then told him as much as she remembered and as much as she had grasped of the conversation with Devi. What sort of business it was going to be with four women in front of computers she had not understood.

"Devi an entrepreneur!" Damodar explained to Malati that she was probably setting up a satellite call centre unit linked to a bigger BPO. It was almost certainly a vernacular service for callers in South Indian languages. It might even be outsourced sales calls, maybe for the chit funds company. There were other possibilities. One thing was certain. Devi had enterprise.

If they were going to help Devi there would have to be many other things done first, many other questions answered. Damodar went into it straight away. Malati was pleased. He got her to write as he dictated a list of things she had to find out about Devi and about the anklet. It would make the job easier at the office when he took it up with the people concerned. Due diligence, he explained.

Malati saw that they had three days before Devi's meeting with Appa on Saturday. She would have to tease out all the bits of information in that time. It had to be a little bit at a time, not all at once, not an interrogation. It had to be in the ten minutes before she left for the 9 o'clock house. Innocent ten minute interviews at a quarter to nine and analytical reports at seven in the evening. That's how it went till the end of the week. On Friday, just before Devi wound up, Malati reminded her that she was to meet Appa the next day, and that she had to bring at least one anklet with her.

⁂ ⁂ ⁂ ⁂ ⁂

Mondays were long days at the bank. Malati was used to Damodar returning only at dinner time. It was nine already. Would he be too tired to talk about the anklet? Would he be in the mood? There was not a word spoken through dinner. When he rose, carrying his plate to the kitchen, he suggested that they talk about it after she had cleared up.

"There are some complications", he began. But first the good news. The single anklet alone was worth at least eight lakhs. Maybe more. A good part of the value came from its age. That was also a part of the complication. Any gold ornament crafted before 1900 carried a premium, but only if it was registered as an heirloom of heritage value. That led to the second complication. The ownership had to be established. It would be very difficult to prove that Devi inherited it from her aunt, already dead. Not impossible, but very difficult and time consuming. The landlord and the temple priest were also dead and gone. The last thing Devi needed was a police verification. If Devi went to the grey market she would get up to a lakh more. But not without the attendant risks.

Malati couldn't help wondering if the chit funds office might help her out. Damodar, now fully with Malati in finding a way out for Devi, would have none of that. Devi's real asset, he explained, was her native intelligence. It was the reason she had not mentioned the anklet at the office. Her liabilities? The wrong combination of caste and class. It was loaded against her. There was no way she would get a fair price for the anklet by herself. She might even... well, there might be a tragic end.

Malati saw that Damodar was looking at her intently. She wondered if his thoughts were the same as hers. Why not put up the anklet for a gold-loan in Malati's name, get the highest possible price for it, and then find a way to pass on the benefit to Devi? Find a way... Damodar had to think about that.

Malati and Damodar started to put things away and lock up. There were footsteps at the staircase. They stopped before their door and the bell rang. Malati fetched a shirt for Damodar. He put it on hurriedly and opened the door.

"Mr. Damodar Raghavan?" It was a police officer. He introduced himself as he let himself in. "Assistant Commissioner Narayan." He was followed by two other officers of lesser rank who stayed at the door while ACP Narayan was led to a seat.

"What can I do for you, Mr...."

"Narayan. From the Crime Branch. Sorry for the late visit, but we had instructions from the Commissioner's office to meet you immediately."

"I see." Damodar tried signaling to Malati to go in, but she remained at the bedroom door, staring. "What is it about?"

"There is an FIR lodged against you. It is in connection with a missing gold anklet."

The Belt

You could say that Hurricane Bhaskaran was a dyed in the wool infantryman. He had served in two of India's wars with the relentlessly hostile neighbor located in the northwest. He had earned two medals for the undaunted pursuit of duty, applying himself to the higher ideals of service. The wars never lasted too long, with both sides running out of ammunition within three weeks. Had they continued longer, Col. Hurricane Bhaskaran might well have covered himself with more decorations.

At this point you will want to know why he was called Hurricane Bhaskaran. It was because he was just that in the boxing ring. Beginning with the first bouts in the featherweight class just before entering college, right through his championship years in the welterweight class, he was nothing short of a hurricane once he stepped into the ring. He was never still. When his fists were held back his feet were prancing restlessly. When they stopped even for a few moments, the fists unleashed a lightning blitz that came from nowhere. He remained a competitive boxer till he was Captain, and hung up his gloves just before being promoted a Major. The moniker remained. It was considered incorrect to call him Hurricane. It was always Hurricane Bhaskaran. Or Colonel Hurricane. A small, select band of those closest to him could call him Hari. That was his first name. In the registers he was Harihar Janardhan Bhaskaran.

All his comrades in the regiment were taken completely by surprise when Col. Bhaskaran announced in the Officers Mess that he was applying for an early voluntary retirement. He was seen as at least Major General material. Why not wait till you are at least a Brigadier, they said. Look at the benefits, they said. Very soon they all accepted that the good Colonel did not wish to talk about it. He spoke at last at the farewell dinner organized by his regiment. What more can one ask for from a life in the army, he began. Battles fought with honour, deep reserves of courage in times of grave danger, unconditional compassion through death and destruction, everlasting comradeship in uniform and out of uniform... The army had given him all that he had dreamed in adolescence. It was as if he had known it all before being selected into the elite regiment, and before the first stripe had been fixed on his epaulette. Now it was time to leave. There were other calls from the wider arena beyond the walls of the regiment. He would cherish every moment of his years in the regiment, every memento presented. That included a shiny new Sam Browne cross belt, given up by the army some years ago, but still held in awe by old soldiers from earlier times. Many still remembered him in the cross belt, the young Major commanding the parade when the Chief of Staff visited the regimental station. How the sabre flashed to the right as he presented his salute to the VIP on the dais! In the privacy of the Commandant's office the Chief had expressed his unqualified admiration for the Major as the very best of the best he had ever seen. The belt was a very special farewell gift indeed.

⁂ ⁂ ⁂ ⁂ ⁂

Out of uniform and into civvies, Hari moved quickly to settle into the new avatar. The choice of city had already been made. It was Bangalore or, more correctly, Bengaluru. Not Bang-a-loru, as the airline cabin crew would say in their announcements. Had he chosen the Cantonment area he might still say Bangalore. He chose instead an area close to his ancestral home, which could only be Bengaluru. It was called Shantiniketan Colony. Settling in included a scouting mission to locate a modest (and affordable) two bedroom house with space for a decent kitchen garden. That was important, not to be compromised. He avoided the word bungalow in his search. He had discovered early that the cost was somehow related closely to the words used in the search.

"I am looking for a small house", he said.

"You mean an independent bungalow?"

"No, no, just a small house."

"With a garden?"

"Some space at the back would be nice. You know, for a tulsi mantap, and hanging clothes."

He never using the word bungalow.

The purchase meant using half his savings up front and taking a housing loan for the remaining amount. Once he and the family of one wife and two children had moved in, the rest of the operations began – the gas cylinder transfer, the telephone connection, the fresh bank account, the house help, the newspaper drop and the standing instructions to the bank for water, telephone and electricity bills. The bank manager had asked about a safe deposit locker for his valuables. Vasantha, the missus, had quipped that his most valuable asset was safe within his rib cage. All through the recce period of about four weeks Hari was also mapping routes for his morning and evening walks.

At last, with all systems ticking, Hari launched his post retirement venture. He would devote himself to educating the youth on health and fitness, concentrating on indigenous health practices. Yes, it included Yoga – not as body contortions, but as a way of life. Not surprisingly the house was named Navodaya.

The garden had most of the essential vegetables for a balanced vegetarian diet, along with a rich mix of greens. It made the maximum use of the available space at the back of the house. In the foreground were rows of root vegetables that needed deeper ground. There were also the bushy varieties like egg plants and ladies fingers. On two sides of the patch was an L-shaped three-tiered structure for the shallower plants. Bunk beds, Hari called them. On the third side were the fruit trees, the guava, chikoo and lime trees. They took ten years to bear fruit. Once they did, the yield was profuse. At one corner were the compost and vermiculture pits, which made the garden complete. The Bhaskarans had a near zero monthly expense at the vegetable market. Some people like to sit in a balcony or verandah facing a patch of lawn in front of the house. They get a ring side view of the street, as they watch the zig-zagging traffic with ever rising anxiety and listen to an infinite variety of horns and beeps. The Bhaskarans had no verandah or lawn. They preferred to sit at the back, watching the flights of butterflies, listening to the twitter of sun birds.

On one side of the colony was a small maidan. It was reserved for a public facility. The Corporation had not decided what the facility would be. Meanwhile it was put to good use by the neighbourhood. Boys played tennis ball cricket in the evenings and holidays. A ladies group gathered there at six in the morning for a laughter work-out. At seven men of all ages gathered there in khaki shorts and black caps, brandishing lathis and fantasizing the destruction of evil forces everywhere. Around that time Hari and his youth brigade would start on their morning jog. As they passed the maidan Hari would be sorely tempted to stop and show the men how to hold a lathi correctly, so that you knocked down a couple of the evil men before being felled yourself by the burst of an assault rifle. Ah, but they knew what they were doing and would not take kindly to advice from a mere soldier.

The young people who gathered at Navodaya, both boys and girls, jogged three mornings a week within the city, and did a hill climb on Sunday mornings. Vasantha had a refreshing glass of fruit juice for them before they set out, and a pile of millet parathas on their return. They ran barefeet. One of the boys went on to become a marathon athlete, still barefeet. Another boy and a girl were prize-winning half marathon runners. For the remaining mornings they had a roster of home visits to help the residents with their own gardens. In less than two years all the homes in the colony had switched to their own vegetables, grown with their own compost. The vegetable vendors were not pleased. People from other colonies swung by to catch a glimpse of birds and butterflies that had disappeared from their parts of town a generation ago. The colony prepared a plan for the Corporation to convert the maidan into a model horticultural garden and resource centre. It would be run as a non-profit Citizens Cooperative. The men in khaki were not pleased.

⌘ ⌘ ⌘ ⌘ ⌘

In no time at all the children had flown out of the nest. The extra room now served other purposes, including that of a guest room. A guest house, really. There were visitors in and out of Navodaya all through the year. It came to be called Col Bhaskaran's Barracks. When the children planned a homecoming Vasantha hurriedly had the extra room cleared and spring cleaned, which was itself a week long project.

Wave after wave of young people had joined Hari Bhaskaran's mission. They had moved on, spending three to four years at Navodaya, but had always stayed in touch. Each wave had spread the gospel with success in different parts of the city. And beyond, when they left Bengaluru to set up home elsewhere.

They called it The Way of Life. Or WOL. It was not Hari who gave the name. It was one of the girls. She even designed a logo, with the silhouetted human figure reaching out to the sun. People called them the organic evangelists. Hari did not like what it implied.

He had no interest in ceremonies and rituals. He took particular care to see that no part of the movement crossed the line and became religious. To regard nature as sacred was crucial, but it was not to be confused with the sacredness of man-made religion. Indeed, you could say that the success of the movement was really in removing layers of confusion from young people's minds. They were replaced with layers of strong scientific curiosity. Once a week, on Thursday evenings (coincidentally the day of the guru), the group engaged in an open discussion of any vexatious issue that had not been addressed satisfactorily elsewhere, in any other social setting, including their schools or colleges. It was an open house evening. Members of the group could bring others along. Anybody could open the discussion with any question brewing in their heads. What is the truth about Ayodhya? Are brahmins more intelligent than others? Why do the poor continue to be poor? Why do girls cry? The rules of the game were set in the earliest meetings. Listening respectfully, no shooting down, one person at a time, and so on. For a whole year the group looked upon Hari for the skilled facilitation needed. Now there were many others who could play the role. Hari sat back.

⌘ ⌘ ⌘ ⌘ ⌘

The three weeks between Dasara and Diwali was the time for the annual family reunion. The family was now one son-in-law, one daughter-in-law and three boys and a girl as grandchildren. "No more", Hari had warned the son and daughter. "The house can't take any more. And we can't be putting you up in hotels."

The extra bedroom was used as a dressing room and for keeping all the bags, most of them on one side of the bed. The other side of the bed was used for short naps by anybody who felt the need for one. The nights were spent on the floor in the living room. It was the best part of the holiday for the children. All the furniture had been moved against the walls. A giant sized dhurry and some extra cotton mattresses had been hired from the shamiana shop. There were enough sheets and pillows in the house. At lights out, announced at 10pm by Hari thata, the entire clan would be on the floor in two rows, the four grown-ups on one side and the four children on the other. It was not unusual for the grandmother to join the children, two of them on either side. The lights out rule did not forbid chattering and joking till all had dropped off one by one. Hari slept in the master bedroom, listening to the chatter and occasionally throwing in a remark himself. There would be a joyous chorus in response from the front room.

It was thirty years since the Bhaskarans had set up their home and Navodaya. The movement had continued, but in other spaces in the city and in other forms. It still served the original purposes of education and civic action. It had flourished without Hari's presence or active involvement. Many had commented that it was the best testimony of the movement's soundness. It had a soul. It was now a registered society. All members knew Hari personally, as they gathered at his home on the last Sunday of every month. And Hari remembered each member by name. The last Sunday during the Dasara-Diwali break had members joining Hari's family at the get-together. There would be many nostalgic moments shared by the older members, especially about the son and daughter who were oh-so-little then. The timing was precise. They would gather at 7 o'clock, just in time to see Hari returning from his evening walk. Vasantha would have the lime juice ready for all.

The evening walk began at six sharp and ended exactly at seven. It was not the distance walked that mattered, but the duration.

Hari was walking shorter distances now. The osteo-arthritis had progressed steadily over the last five years and had slowed him down. It had not stopped him. The increasing volume of traffic and the accompanying irresponsible driving habits of car owners had made him even slower. It had not stopped him. He was well prepared.

The groundwork for the walk began at a quarter to six, exactly fifteen minutes before he stepped out of the front door. Vasantha laid out all his requirements around a table next to the armchair by half past five. The family had gathered for the afternoon tea and snacks. The goodies they had brought were supplemented with fresh muffins baked by Vasantha. Hari proceeded with his preparation through their animated babble.

He first wore the knee length white socks with the two bands of blue above. After both socks were worn he stood up and tested the correctness of stretch around the ankles and calves. Next, seated again, he pulled on the ankle length canvas boots, one boot at a time, but left them unlaced. He would return to them later. Standing once more, he wore his two-sided jerkin, the green side out, zipping up to five inches from the top. Over the jerkin he slipped on the sleeveless jacket with the horizontal fluorescent bands at the back and front. It got dark rapidly after half past six, and fast moving cars had to see a moving figure on one side of the road where there were no pavements. He then put on the helmet and strapped up. It was a gleaming white motorcycle head gear that was modeled after the Military Police helmet of the same colour. It had a luminous red band going round an inch above the rim. He then sat down and tucked the ends of his trousers into the boots and laced them up. He rose again and did a few stretches, turning left and right at the waist, touching the floor, loosening his shoulders and hugging his knees one by one. He put on a pair of anti-glare glasses in a gold plated frame. He paused for a few moments, looking ahead, waiting for his eyes to adjust to the lenses. He then slipped on a pair of white gloves. He practiced his hand signals with the gloves on, so important on the walk. Finally, he added the last item to his walking gear. He wore the Sam Browne cross belt over the jacket, pulling in his waist and buckling up. The clock struck six when he stepped out.

Vasantha had cleared up and got the family to agree on the dinner menu. The lime juice was ready. She looked at her watch. It was seven already. She looked at the front gate expecting to see Hari entering. He must have stopped at the end of the road, she thought. He did that sometimes to chat up the little boy walking his dog. The dog was always happy to see Hari and wanted his share of attention. Vasantha stepped out of the gate to join them herself. There was nobody there. Ah, well, she said to herself. Why should he not be making new friends on his walk. He would be home any minute. It was less than a minute. A dozen motorcycles and cars were zooming toward the house. Behind them was an ambulance, the siren blaring. And behind the ambulance, more cars, more two-wheelers, and hundreds of people on foot. They were all headed to Navodaya. It was the last Sunday of the month.

The First Offering

Crouching on the cold stone floor in the police lock-up with an ache in every limb was not the happy ending to the week Ramji Maharaj had planned. He should have been on the mofussil bus by now, well past the octroi check post, where Gori would join him after her weekly offering at the Ambaji shrine.

Oh... the pain in the legs. Above the knees, below, everywhere. The havildar's lathi was deadly accurate in landing exactly where he seemed to want it. He looked like a friendly doodhwala when he came to Bhabiji's place in response to her phone call. He smiled a lot. He thought the doodhwala was on his side. But when his palm rested at the back of the neck it was a grip that spoke another language. On reaching the thana the Havildar had assured Ramji that his stay would be short. It was a little formality. The lathi ran a quick burst of strokes, merely a warm-up, and mainly to satisfy Bhabiji that something had been done.

⌘ ⌘ ⌘ ⌘ ⌘

Ramji raised his head as a dog would at the first sense of unfamiliar footsteps.

"Oi, there is someone to see you!"

The sight of the doodhwala, now grinning earlobe to earlobe, slowed his straightening up noticeably.

"Is this the way to receive your gharwali? Here, you can talk to her. She has asked for you anyway."

"Gori? How did she...?"

"We found her. Part of the job. We posted a constable outside the bungalow. She got there soon enough."

"Bhabiji's bungalow?"

"Some kothi, perhaps?"

"Look here, you have no..."

"Yes?" It was that smile again.

"Nothing". Ramji was quite awake now. He wondered if Gori was also under arrest.

"No, she is not. She went to a temple. We checked that. She has some prasad for you."

Ramji looked up at the havildar, and looked down again. The havildar answered the question unasked.

"She has not been touched. There is no need. It is a silly chota-mota case. A nuisance. But we have to attend to it when there is a complaint from bungalow people."

Bungalow people. The same people who had slammed the door when the neighbourhood boys had gone seeking a token chanda for Ganesh Chaturthi. Given half a chance they would have all the Ramjis and Goris of the city rounded up and sent off to the Andamans. Who will do the jhadu-potha-kapda then? What had Ramji done anyway? What did Bhabiji mean when she said he had brought ruination to the house with his wickedness? The havildar decided to ask Ramji about it the next morning.

⌘ ⌘ ⌘ ⌘ ⌘

It was simply a belly need. Ramji began on his story after the havildar had shared his roti and garlic chutney with him. He had slept surprisingly well. His favourite dream of the anthill next to a peepal tree had reappeared, and he was at peace with himself. The aches in his arms and legs were seeking less attention.

Bhabiji simply should not have come into the kitchen at that time.

What was he doing at that time? Well, resting, as any hardworking maharaj might be, after a long morning that ends only at three in the afternoon. What was the problem? Was he expected to be doing something else?

"There were two problems. I was smoking a cigarette. And I was bare-chested."

"Only your chest?"

"No, it wasn't what you think."

"Bungalow people!"

"I jumped up and tried to get my shirt, but it was too late."

It was a foreign cigarette, a lone stick lying untouched on a tray at the garden party the previous night. Ramji tried to explain that he had just found it there. But she didn't give him a chance.

"Ramji, you are supposed to be a Brahman. That is how you got to be appointed maharaj in this household. Do you smoke?"

Ramji fumbled for an answer. He was not really a smoker. Three bidis a day were a luxury. Cigarettes? Only if somebody offered one. The foreign cigarette had been too much of a temptation. And it had been abandoned on the tray. Bhabhiji cut in again.

"And where is your thread? How can you be a Brahman and not have your thread on?"

Ramji tried again to explain. After his bath he'd hung up the thread to dry. He knew himself it was not convincing. She had him trapped. She asked the pointed question. Was he or was he not a Brahman? With some difficulty and with some anticipation of what was to come Ramji admitted that he was not one. So, how did he dare to say that he was a Brahman when he came to seek the job?

Ramji found himself blurting out the truth. "It was simply a belly need. I had to stoop to even this, being a Brahman, so that my wife and I could have two meals a day."

Bhabiji's face changed colour three times in three seconds. The manner of her exit suggested that something terrible was going to happen. It happened with the arrival of the havildar. She was the wife of the businessman in the white safari suit, the white shoes and the gold bracelet. Over the fifty years since independence the thana had learned to pay special attention to people dressed in dazzling white.

⌘ ⌘ ⌘ ⌘ ⌘

A chota-mota case. As if the thana didn't have enough on its hands. The extortion of pavement dwellers by the druggies, the streetwalkers being organized against the pimps, the elections round the corner... street crime and violence they could handle with their eyes closed, but elections – that was another category of headache altogether.

On the bicycle ride home to the police lines the havildar kept thinking of the election tamasha in the city. On the face of it, the whole thing was some sort of madness. How could God's own children behave this way at election time? What people will not do for a little bit more in their pockets. The jackals piling into the lorries for slogan shouting were probably victims of their own shortsightedness. But how could big people, educated people, get sucked into such a pathetic state? Merchants, factorywallas, ministers, their families, even government officers. He had seen them all, going round and round like street dogs in season. They could be as vicious if you crossed their path. In the season, more than at any other time, dogs marked their territories with the greatest fervour.

He had just reached the turning for the police lines when a gleaming white car, long and low, lunged past the amber light, wiggling its bottom at the others who had chosen to stop. In it was a man in a white safari suit. Why, it was the businessman! Bhabiji's businessman husband. The dark glasses in the gold plated frame served more to highlight his identity than to conceal it. It was like that with all in dark glasses – the cinema star, the politician, the minister, the smuggler. Maybe it was a caste mark of some kind.

They came without warning, from behind the puffs of white clouds. Just as the havildar was storing the mental image of the face in the dark glasses, a routine that came naturally to him, he saw in the sky a formation of gigantic men, all in white, all in dark glasses. All of them had their palms pressed together in front of themselves. They were smiling uniformly, knowingly, at the multitudes below.

The havildar looked about. All around him he saw the mass stupor of the six o'clock traffic brought to standstill. He dismounted, turned his bicycle around, pushed it past the cars, two-wheelers, auto rickshaws and other contraptions, and started pedaling again. When the road in front of him was clear, he looked back briefly. The sky had cleared. The multitudes had returned to chaotic normalcy.

⌘ ⌘ ⌘ ⌘ ⌘

When the Havildar reached the thana, Ramji had just been released and allowed to go. His wife had brought him a snack and some tea. They were startled when they saw the figure of the havildar against the arched entrance. When he stepped in from the light they saw that he was not smiling. With a quick businesslike wave of his lathi he motioned them to be seated on the bench and walked briskly past them into the Superintendent's office. When he emerged a minute later it was with another wave of his lathi, this time directing them into the interrogation room. Once in, he closed the door behind him and stood there, feet planted firmly a foot and a half apart, his hands locked behind his back, the lathi tucked into his left armpit. He stared at Ramji and Gori, shifting his gaze from one to the other, and finally resting it on Gori. He smiled.

How did a woman with the complexion of seasoned teak get the name Gori, the Havildar wanted to know.

Ramji dared to smile in return. "We should ask her", he suggested.

"Nobody in the family really knows. Some think it is actually the goddess Gowri. Others think that next to the two sisters with the complexion of seasoned rosewood my father thought I should be called Gori".

"That is fine" said the Havildar. "That is just fine. The name Gowri suits you well. And you, Ramji bhaiya, you could also do with a change of name... a change of clothes... a change in address..."

He let these out one by one, savouring each pause, and dropping his voice further each time. He drew Ramji and Gori to the corner of the room and got them to sit in a tight huddle with him.

"Listen carefully". The havildar looked at the two of them intently. They could only nod silently. They were placing their lives in his hands. "This is not an interrogation." There was the faintest grin on Ramji's face. He looked at Gori. She responded with an unspoken admonition. The havildar spoke reassuringly. "How can we have justice if we don't have God on our side?"

⌘ ⌘ ⌘ ⌘ ⌘

With the help of the stand-in maharaj loaned for an hour a day by her sister-in-law, an arrangement not without ripple effects in the already strained cordiality between the two households, Bhabiji managed to serve a frugal evening meal, compensated with a do-it-yourself green salad. Her businessman husband and she sat at the two ends of their ten-seater dining table, which was the respected custom, and ate their dinners in silence, which was the accepted practice. Watching him from the top of her spectacles Bhabiji noticed that the furrows on his brow were deeper than usual. The grating sound at his end of the table was from his teeth. She had a sudden fear that the husband might break tradition and speak at the meal. The businessman cleared his throat and mumbled a half sentence that sounded distinctly like half a curse. Well, if he could break tradition, so could she. She voiced a half question. "You were saying...?"

"There is a temple on the land".

"A temple?"

"That's what I said, didn't I?" He was not used to being interrupted.

"Which land? Oh, you mean...?"

"Yes, our land. Next to the corporation maidan. A small shrine below the peepal tree. But all the jhopdi people in that area call it their temple."

⌘ ⌘ ⌘ ⌘ ⌘

The havildar sat opposite his wife for his favourite evening meal of hot khichdi, red pumpkin kadhi and buttermilk. She had laid on a bonus dish, a green salad, arranged the way she had seen in a TV programme. She was so happy that they could eat together. It had become more and more difficult in recent times, especially after his promotion. The 2-in-1 was playing his favourite cassette, the dialogue from the movie Sholay. He seemed in such a good mood too. She hoped he would make some jolly conversation. The havildar asked her to turn off the 2-in-1. There was something very funny he wanted to tell her. She jumped up and put the machine off. This was going to be like old times, the stories he brought home from the beat.

"You know the rule. This is only between the two of us. Strictly." She nodded readily and enthusiastically. "Which means...?"

"Not even in my dreams", she completed the sentence for him. She placed her hand on his thigh, the muscles bulged from his sitting cross-legged on the floor. He patted her hand, as if to say, good girl. It was their special hand on hand on thigh contact that communicated in the instant what all the film songs from Bombay put together could not.

"You know the new political party that has come up? The one with the peepal leaf as its symbol? They are going to win the seat for this part of the city."

"Party? Election? I thought you were going to..."

The havildar looked at her puzzled face and laughed so hard that he had hiccups. She rose to fetch him some drinking water, but he held her back.

"It is the old story of the monkey and the snake and the rat and the tiger trapped in a well, along with the thief from the city. There is a certain bhai bhai air among them that all of them know is short-lived. Each will try to use another to get out of the well. Afterwards, each creature will display its real appetites."

"Yes, I remember. Go on". She realized that he had been switched on. Interruptions were not in order, even if she was not following things quite so clearly.

"The politician, the businessman, the local goonda, the governmentwalla, the lawyer, yes, he too – when they get together you see the strangest happenings. Especially at election time."

"Who is the monkey in this group?"

The havildar laughed again. She was so beautiful when she asked such questions. He realized his hiccups had gone.

"There is a peepal tree at the edge of the Corporation maidan."

"I know, the one with an anthill next to it."

"Yes, that one. There is now a temple next to the anthill."

"A temple? I thought it took at least twenty years to build a temple."

"There are some that take twenty years. Some take two hundred years. But you can also do something through one night in about two hours. A place of worship is a place of worship, whether it is built in two hundred years or in two hours."

"Is there an idol in the shrine? Which god resides in there?"

That smile again. She topped up the steel tumbler with more buttermilk.

"What more can the citizens of this locality ask for? It is a Ganesh temple. It is the first auspicious happening in their lives."

She was accustomed to the havildar's storytelling style, but this one was going over her head. Cautiously, taking care to show continued interest, she began clearing up. The havildar asked teasingly if she would like to make an offering at the new Ganesh temple. How could she not, she replied instantly. She would get ready at once.

But who would accept the offering? And who would perform the puja? Why, the temple priest, of course.

"A priest at the shrine already?"

"Yes. His name is Ganesh Maharaj. His wife is called Gowri Mata. The people in the locality went from jhopdi to jhopdi and took a collection to build a small one room home for them next to the shrine."

"On that land? Does it not belong to that businessman in the huge bungalow with four cars?"

"Does it? Does it not belong to the Corporation? I suppose we will never know. But how does it matter? The land is blessed by the presence of Lord Ganesh himself now."

"I am sure you are right. But I can't help being afraid."

"You don't need to be. The Corporation and the businessman need each other."

"They can get together then to have the land cleared."

"And both of them need the leader of the peepal leaf party. They want him to win in this election."

"What? That ugly man with the long list of cases against him? How can he win? How can he even stand for election?"

"The people decide that. Not you and me."

"But what if..."

"If what? You think you are living in a jungle? This is a civilized society, with a long and glorious history."

"I know, I know", she replied in some exasperation, "the long line of great rulers from the Guptas to the Gandhis." She slipped into the adjoining room to get ready.

Meanwhile, the havildar washed his thali and the two tumblers, changed quickly out of uniform, and waited in the centre of the room. When she reappeared, she was wearing the sari the havildar had given her at the last Ganesh Chaturthi festival. In her hands was the silver tray her mother had given her at their wedding. They stood at their places looking at each other. Her anxiety seemed to have receded as she playfully scolded him.

"Are we going to stand here all night staring at each other? The temple doors will close. We still have to pick up flowers and a coconut."

He stepped up to her and held her face in his hands. Looking into his eyes, it was easier for her to ask the question that had crossed her mind.

"Are you in any way involved in all this?"

The large reassuring smile returned on the havildar's face. He replied in the gently firm tone she understood so well.

"All I can do is help a little bit... to bring Lord Ganesh into the lives of godless people."

[This is the very first short story. It was written during the time there was a mushrooming of shrines on roadsides and in vacant sites with no action over them.]

The Bungalow

In the old days the posting meant something else. It meant being both a Collector and a Magistrate. The post had power. I remember my grandfather telling me about the powers he had as a District Collector, who also had to serve as a District Magistrate. It could go to your head. It did, for some people. It didn't for most. They learned soon enough that the best way to govern a District was for people to see the power you carried in you all the time, but not feel it beating down their backs. The appurtenances of power were more important than their use. The ivory handle of the pistol sticking out of the holster on your hip was an example, even if the people never saw it fired. Today it is the sheathed flag on the bonnet of the Ambassador, even if it is never seen fluttering.

By the time my father joined the service the magisterial responsibilities were separated into another line. He was just a Collector. What he collected was never understood by his children, the three of us, my two sisters and I, but we knew he had a large collection of stories. As a ten year old I was satisfied with that explanation. My father was a Collector of stories. They were about dacoits roaming in the woods, the merchants in the small town who were looted by the dacoits, the humble folks in the villages cheated by the merchants, the panthers and foxes stalking their cattle and chickens, and the city folks descending on the District in hunting parties. The black buck doe was a prized target. It gave you the very best venison. There was no ban on hunting in the wild those days.

When we heard the gate open and the Willys station wagon roared in we stopped whatever we were at and rushed in to freshen up and assemble in the drawing room. Amma put the kettle on for fresh chai. The chaprasi would enter first and place Appa's files on the corner table. Appa would then come in and drop into his favourite sofa and sign some papers for the chaprasi to take back. Amma and the three children would then enter from two directions and sit around him. He would smile at us indulgently, showing he was tired, but he would clear his throat nevertheless and begin, "You know what happened yesterday..."

You will know by now that we are a family of Collectors. At least one in every generation has been in the Service from the time it was called Imperial Civil Service. In earlier times, with the family size often exceeding six, it was not unusual for a brother to be a colleague too. Some families produce doctors, some lawyers. We produced Collectors.

The bungalow was at least a hundred years old. It had a double-door iron gate between two lengths of railway line buried deep into the ground and cemented. The railings and the gate were painted white. The gate was heavy. There was a coat of white paint for every year of its life. On either side of the gate was a wire fence within which was a croton hedge, the fence and hedge covering three sides of the compound. The boughs of two gulmohar trees formed a welcome arch above the gate. Inside the gate was a circular gravel path, wide enough for a motor car leading to a covered portico. It was customary to enter taking the left path and leave from the right. The compound space was vast. The bungalow itself was painted a distinctly deep terra-cotta. The locals called it Lal Bangla.

The bungalow had a spacious drawing room, a separate dining room, three bedrooms, a guest room and a study. But it looked tiny from the road, set inside the large and pretty compound. A wide verandah, raised four feet above the gravel path, was where the Sahib met people with their petitions once a week.

The verandah had the original tiled roofing above. If you looked carefully you would see the rings and hinges of the original pankha that was operated by a servant seated on a modha at one end of the verandah. Within the circular path was a lawn surrounded by flower beds and a small fountain in the centre that also functioned as a bird bath. On either side of the path were fruit trees. Most first time Collectors had their first taste of bel fruit and its famed sherbet in this house. The jamun tree on the opposite side, not to be outdone by the bel, greeted visitors with a lush carpet of indigo below and a copious supply above that was the fleshiest and juiciest you would ever have tasted. At the back were quarters for the servants on one side, which included an ex-army driver. On the other side was a double garage, once used for a horse carriage. Only two ornate wheels and a pair of suspension leaf springs remained. They were kept covered by a sheet of tarpaulin on one side and dusted and lightly oiled the first Sunday of every month. Their presence was verified once a year by the bungalow inventory inspection.

We were all taught riding at the Academy. We had to pass a test too. Nobody mounted any beast of the horse family of equidae in any posting thereafter. One exception I can think of was a batch-mate of mine who was posted in the Madhya Pradesh cadre. An angry crowd of protestors put him on a donkey and paraded him from his home to the railway station, advising him to take the next train out of town. The Lal Bangla garage was now occupied by an early model of Hindustan Ambassador, maintained in immaculate condition by the workshop of the District Police Centre. The space at the rear was meant entirely for a vegetable garden.

As you might guess there was a move to bring down the bungalow and put up a block of apartments to house six families. Successive Collectors had thwarted the move for over twenty years, applying one argument or the other, citing one clause or another from government documents to which only they seemed to have access. All it needed was a decision to appoint another Committee to examine the issue afresh. Each Collector wished only for the Committee to meet after his term was over and he moved to another assignment. If you have ever lived in a brick and mortar bungalow with walls a foot and a half thick, you will know why the Collectors did not wish to give it up. Cool in summer, warm in winter, with a generous supply of fruit and vegetables the year round, you would never want to give it up for a concrete pill box.

Bungalows all over the country were replaced steadily by pill boxes. They had to go. Lal Bangla was an exception. It stayed for two reasons. It was a District posting nobody wanted. People in the Service called it by different names, boondocks, badlands, hellsink, and so on. People in the State capital avoided any reference to the District, lest they be directed to make a field visit. They preferred to let the District administration administer itself, always remembering to record what a splendid job the boys had done.

The second reason is difficult to explain. It is difficult for people brought up in the cities to grasp. The bungalow, you see, had a soul. No, more than that, it was a living body. You will laugh at me. You will close the story immediately.

If you do, you will have missed a lesson in the science of life that they do not teach you in the city schools. You see, we know that the soul of a person in the afterlife leaves one body and settles in another just coming to life. Ah, but in our arrogance we think the human soul can settle only into another human body. Why should it not settle into a dog? A frog, an ant? Why not into a tree, a river? Are they not all alive? A bullock cart, is it not alive? And a house? When all the parts are joined together with one last piece put into place, it comes to life, does it not? Does it not acquire a character of its own? A house too can have its own life. A foundation below, the walls on the sides, a roof above, the windows bringing in sunlight, a hearth to keep it warm – when you light a fire the first time in the kitchen, there is life in the body. If you have reached this far, I can take it that you wish to know more.

⁂

It is said that the first white man sent to this part of the country to tame the natives and to get them to pay taxes was a Scotsman by the name of James McKenzie. He was indeed the first Collector and District Magistrate. It was he who built Lal Bangla, then known as Makkhanji Bangla. He lived in a large tent a mile down the dirt track. It also served as his field office. Breaking custom, he had his young wife join him there. Sarah Parker was her name. A young Collector, a young bride, a first posting, you see, they were setting a trend. She joined him almost directly from the ship, with just a day's rest with the Company community in the port city. She took charge of the bungalow construction immediately, spending the day at the site and the night in the tent. Alas, Sarah mem-sahib was stricken with malaria, accompanied by convulsive high fever, and she died before the foundation was fully in place. A grief-stricken McKenzie buried her in one corner of the site, and with a determination that the natives could attribute only to a Scotsman, he completed the first small bungalow within the month, laying the bricks himself along with the coolies. People passing by in the dark often heard McKenzie talking to somebody inside the room in a quiet whisper. Some swear that they heard a female voice in conversation with him.

James and Sarah loved each other deeply. He swore he would not look at another woman with desire, and she swore complete faithfulness to him. These vows were necessary, you see, because life was not easy for young couples posted in mofussil areas.

Tours in the countryside and trips to the Presidency offices had long periods of separation and loneliness that affected both the men and the women.

The Company permitted McKenzie an extended furlough to recover from his grief. When he returned, he carried with him a life sized portrait of Sarah in a gilded frame. There was a quiet ceremony attended by the local gentry and his superior from Headquarters. He met the group on the verandah. This time it was for the unveiling. The gathering did not know how to react when he had the portrait taken inside and hung on the wall opposite the fireplace. He succeeded in breaking the silence by leading the group in a short prayer, which ended with an earnest wish for Sarah to remain the loving guardian of the Bungalow, as she always wanted to be.

He then added a line only by himself, reminding Sarah that their vows to each other were eternal. The local pandit held up a lamp to light the portrait. Sarah, now brought to life, was seen smiling serenely in benediction.

The night watchman slipped out of the gathering after the prasad had been distributed by the pandit. He took his place at the gate, and shared the prasad with his wife who had chosen to remain outside. She had caught a glimpse of the portrait on the wall through a half-opened window and was stunned by the beauty of Sarah mem-sahib in the gilded frame. She was convinced that she had read the mem-sahib's heart the way only another woman could. Makkhanji-sahib would never understand the half of it. The house was indeed Sarah mem-sahib in another form. She would take care of the sahib as long as he remained there. She would bring peace and harmony and eternal love within the body of the house. More, she would make sure that true justice prevailed in the soul of the bungalow, from where the sahib would take care of the land and its peoples.

McKenzie had a pair of fine horses. He could either ride them singly on his field trips or tether them as a pair to draw his carriage to headquarters. He liked to do all his field work by himself, and on horseback. No servants, no chaprasi, no fuss. It was not unusual for him to be away for two or three nights at a stretch. He gave his time to all villages in the district in equal measure, treating all of the communities fairly and without prejudice. It was only a village across the river that seemed to take more of his time. It was a clutch of five hamlets, but treated as one village in the revenue records. It was a forested area and isolated from the rest of the District. He always took a little longer returning from the village across the river. There was the not unexpected whispered talk about MacKenzie-sahib and the village.

McKenzie stopped at the stream to rest awhile before crossing it for the last stretch home. He allowed the horse to cool itself in the stream and settled himself in the shade of a fig tree. He loosened his belt, unbuttoned his shirt and leaned back against the tree. He took out his leather bound diary from his breast pocket as he was used to doing whenever he was by himself. The diary had a picture of Sarah. He checked himself and put the diary on the ground beside him. Just then he saw his horse straightening himself. He stood on his hind legs and whinnied and stomped his forelegs on the ground, rose again and whinnied some more, louder than ever. The horse then bolted away, galloping in frenzy towards the village he had just come from. McKenzie straightened himself to size up the situation. It was too late. An enormous rock python had slid up the arm resting on the ground. In a flash it had entwined itself around his waist and was now staring into his ashen face.

A group of six villagers armed with lathis and choppers arrived. They saw a half swallowed Makkhanji-sahib inside a python that seemed to be taking a rest break. His head and neck were gone, and the chest had been crushed to the girth of a narrow drainpipe. Five of the villagers advanced on the python cautiously to see what might be done. One of them stood back, his head lowered, but watching intently. It was not easy extricating the body, recognizable only by the trousers and boots. They wiped the slimy remains as best as they could with tendu leaves. The foul smell remained. They wrapped the upper half tightly with whatever cloth they could spare from their own garments. They made a light bier with bamboos and carried the body back to the bungalow. The horse followed at a distance. The villager who had held back was rooted to the spot.

A messenger was despatched to Headquarters with the news. McKenzie's superior arrived the next day, accompanied by a chaplain, not before the body had decomposed further. A Christian burial was hastily arranged. An enquiry was commissioned immediately, and the bungalow was sealed.

⁂ ⁂ ⁂ ⁂ ⁂

The story of McKenzie and Sarah mem-sahib amused some and frightened others. Even when I joined the Service, which must have been a hundred years later, or more, the story was part of my induction ceremony. There were many versions, of course, each with its own mirch-masala. Members of the Officers Club at Headquarters loved to ply a newcomer with story after story about the McKenzies. They even had a cocktail called James' Flame. When Nalini arrived to join me at the District, and there was the customary welcome party at the Club, I found the time to give her a pre-induction trailer before the blitz. A young bride just arriving in the District could so easily be pounced upon.

The holidaying was soon over, and the field trips resumed. The fact is that when you are on a field trip you can't help thinking of all the stories blowing freely through the district all the time – the wandering minstrels and their all-night camps, the rascals from the small town raiding the protected forests, the cow elephant guarding her calf from the prowling tigress, the big breasted village woman suckling an orphaned baby deer, the fight to death between the mongoose and the cobra, dying in each other's embrace, the soothsayer fakir who arranged bridegrooms for girls on their puberty... Stories from the District. The dak bungalow caretakers had their own share of tales to entertain you. Sometimes, when it is exceptionally late, and the nearest dak bungalow is more than an hour's drive away, you can rest under the stars in a sleeping bag, the trusty Ambassador just a few feet away. It is then you recall the story of James McKenzie and Sarah.

I had the Ambassador, sometimes with a driver, sometimes without one, but it did not make the field trips any shorter. District administration is far more complicated now than in the old days. It is not uncommon for the tours to be five whole days. Nalini was getting used to the life of a District Collector's wife.

I knew a transfer was being talked about at Headquarters. It was due. My time at the District was coming to an end. The fresh posting would probably be a deemed promotion as well. It would be good to sink my teeth into a new responsibility. But I would miss the bungalow. If only I could spend more time there, enjoying the calm and beauty of the surroundings, and not keep wandering all over the District.

It was a clear sky above. The cool breeze swirling around me kept me awake, but it was blissful. I could have spent the whole night counting the stars, and with each star I recognized I could count a blessing in my life. There were so many stars to count. I decided to get into the car and drive. It was just over one at night. I was wide awake. If I drove carefully, stopping to splash water on my face every half hour or so I should be home well before dawn.

The engine responded smartly to the touch of the starter, reading my mind, and I was off. Fifteen minutes to get off the dirt track and I would be on the narrow District road heading home. The bungalow was in sight from half a mile away. The gul mohar arch glowed in the early streaks of light in the eastern sky. The watchman had gone home to catch some sleep. I stopped in front of the gate to open it. As I stepped out I saw a Premier-Fiat parked at the portico. Kishore? In the house? I then saw a light on in the bedroom. I also heard agonized wailing from the drawing room in front, still dark. I decided to leave the car at the gate and walk down to the house. I stepped in cautiously, not knowing what to expect, yet expecting something terrible.

In the dimness I could see Kishore in a heap, wailing, sobbing convulsively, disheveled, his shirt in his hands in a tight bundle, bent. A heap.

I switched on the light. He did not look up. I called out to him softly. He raised his head, very slowly, half expecting me to be there. He said nothing. He raised his hand next, pointing to the bedroom. I waited a while, not knowing if I should rush to him first or look into the adjoining room. Seeing Kishore's distressed state I decided to go where he was pointing.

It was the most terrifying sight I have ever seen in all my life. Nalini was on the floor. One arm was on a pillow at the edge of the bed, her hand clinging it tightly, tearing the cover. Half her sari was on the floor. Her body was twisted, her face was contorted. One leg was pulled up to her belly. The other was under the armchair next to the bed. I did not have to reach her to know that she was quite dead. I did not know immediately what the connection to Kishore was, but I sensed a deep and powerful anger swell up inside me. I was going to pick up the armchair, raise it all the way up above my head and bring it down to smash Kishore's skull with it. It was then that I saw the cobra. It was dark brown, thick and flat as all the really dangerous ones are, easily six feet long. It had coiled itself around Nalini's leg and was staring at me, the hood half raised, daring me to take another step.

...

The Calling

You want to talk to me about the Gang of Six? You are not the first, you know. What is there to say? Yes, I know them. Yes, they are good friends. But you can see I am busy now. You see that, don't you? I am about to leave. I have to pick up some things they need, and some hot food and some fruits. Yes, we can talk as we walk down the stairs. You can come with me to the supermarket. No further than that, I am afraid. They won't allow that. You will understand that they are not convicted. Not yet. They were arrested and are in custody. That is different. They are lodged in two different locations, the two women in a special Police Station in Indiranagar for women offenders. It sounds funny, doesn't it? Women offenders. So does Indiranagar? Well, you said that, not I. Make sure you don't put words in my mouth. Go ahead, ask questions. I will do my best to help you. There is nothing to hide. But for god's sake don't add more masala than what's already been dumped by the other papers. It's awful.

⁂ ⁂ ⁂ ⁂ ⁂

They met every Friday. We called them the Jumma Mubarak group. Not one of the six in the group was Muslim. Otherwise it was as diverse a group as it could possibly get. But no Muslim. Nevertheless, it was called the Jumma Mubarak group. Or simply JM. They had hoped that Javed would join. It was not to be. He was constantly on stand by at the office for weekend delivery trips to Mumbai. He remained a close friend, but was not JM. I almost joined the group myself, but Friday evening meetings were ruled out. It was the evening reserved for my in-laws. It was usually a film on DVD in their grand home theatre set up. Sometimes when the movie got boring I would wonder what the JM group was up to at that moment. I married early. The group could not be expected to know the burden of obligations on the shoulders of one recently married. Only one other in the circle of friends had this marital status, which meant being neither here nor there. We were part of the group, but still not part of it. It was understood that we were different. Exactly how nobody knew.

The arrangement worked perfectly. The small office belonged to Noshir-kaka who ran a financial advisory service. Their work was usually over by half past five every evening. The small team of five hung on for about half an hour attending to personal mails and phone calls. On Fridays the JMs walked in at six with hot bataka vadas or samosas for all. After the snacks and chai Noshir-kaka's team left and the office became the JM adda. They took care of the locking up, informing the caretaker on the ground floor when they left.

You will ask: what did the Jumma Mubarak group do? They wrote. They were like columnists, writing occasionally in news magazines and quite regularly in the Sunday edition of The National Post. I can tell you they were not writers of the garden variety. They had to be up there to be writing for The Post. They had a wide readership and were highly respected. The difference was that they wrote as a team. They signed off as Shukria, a single name. The name could mean either the Urdu thank you or a Friday offering. Only the families and some very close friends knew that Shukria was the JM Group. Most readers did not know that it was a group. Individual names were never given anywhere, any time.

Every essay by Shukria was acclaimed as sharp and incisive writing. It was based on in-depth research and analysis and the presentation was lucid. It was never a bombast. It took the reader for a quiet walk along a stream and opened the eyes to the wondrous reality in the flow, often succeeding in getting people to confront prejudices and contradictions carried for many years in their lives. It never resorted to clever word play, the trick journalists employ when short on facts. Who can forget the landmark essay on garbage titled The Earthworm, in which Shukria got readers to see that "the garbage problem" was not in its unsatisfactory clearing, but in its creation in the first place. Why do we produce so much garbage? And the even more difficult question, why do we consume so much that we must produce so much garbage? The group had conducted a successful field experiment in a locality of a hundred households to show that the most effective garbage management solution was in producing as little garbage as possible.

⌘ ⌘ ⌘ ⌘ ⌘

The writing came easily to the JM group because they were all researchers at heart. Knowledge workers, we call them. It was in their professions. Do you want me to tell you more about the group? I suppose it should not matter. Not anymore. It is all out anyway. The media has gone crazy on the case. I suppose you have read all kinds of reports already on the Gang of Six, as they have come to be called now. A lot of it cooked up to keep the gossip going, extracting the last drop for mileage from the story, knowing that it cannot last more than the standard run of five days before the next sensational story breaks out. Let me tell you about them anyway.

Venky, a Tambram (Palghat to boot), was a media planner in the country's second largest advertising and communications agency. Eddie, Eduljee in his school leaving certificate, was a financial analyst, and as the nephew of Noshir-kaka, understood the intricacies of the most complex fiscal systems in Indian businesses. George Kurien, GK, led the young operations research team in a large but low profile export marketing firm. The chemical technology whizz was Thambi. There was nothing he did not know about recycling and reuse. The shirts he wore were from yarn made from discarded packing cartons. The two women in the group were A2 and Tina, both techies in the IT industry. Aditi Appiah had moved from customer relationship to business development in the country's fastest growing second tier IT company. Christina Mendes was a quality and process engineering specialist and the most sought after person in the field by headhunting agencies. That was the JM group. All for one and one for all as Shukria. They loved writing.

⌘ ⌘ ⌘ ⌘ ⌘

It all began with a thought provoking but funny piece on the subject of morality in Indian public life. The uncomplicated line of reasoning was that there were two steady trends observed in India over twenty five years. It seemed to originate in the early 'nineties. One was the slow but clear decline in morality. The second was a slow but clear increase in religiosity. The first was assessed through five main domains of social conduct. A Social Morality Index was derived from the five dimensions. The second was assessed through observable and measurable increases in ritual religious behavior. Most interesting for readers was the increase in expenditure in different kinds of religious behavior, teased out from market data – from sales of Ganesha idols to pujas at shrines for new purchases. Then came the question: Were the two trends related in some way? The decline in morality and the rise in religiosity? The readership response was unprecedented. The polarization of responses was predictable.

This led to a three-part series on the subject, aptly titled The Great Indian Mask. It should have ended there. That was my opinion, as well as that of other friends of JM. The group agreed, but felt that the three essays and the huge volume of readership views had thrown up so much interesting new material that a follow up set was called for. The mopping up set, Eddie said with his toothy grin. As suggested by both Venky and A2 the next set of essays would be constructed as a fresh piece. The Mask series would be shown as closed. If readers saw the new topic as an extension of the Mask, well, they were free to do so. Not surprisingly, they did.

The new series was titled Heritage. The title and the first two paragraphs of the opening essay were hooks. It made the reader feel good about India's uniquely rich cultural history and included nuggets of details from the Harappan era that made the reader proud of one's roots in the Indian sub-continent. It was educative, beginning with the root civic in understanding civilizations, and the extraordinary advances in public systems in the Indus Valley. Water and sanitation, food storage and distribution, education and training, construction technology, metallurgy, weaponry, these were all well ahead of their times. The essay won over the newly emerging readership of Nationalists by suggesting that the richness existed well before the Aryan arrival, and that Western writers on ancient Indian history might have got it wrong. It also chastised them for ignoring the ancient civilizations in the Southern part of the sub-continent.

The second part of the essay zeroed in on a critical idea. It showed places of worship as the most complete representation of a civilization and a culture at any time. It presented examples, a mere small sample, of great temple architecture as expressions of highly developed cultures in every corner of the land. It ended with a short participatory exercise for reader involvement. Shukria invited readers to send in names of places of worship that they would list as culturally important. The places of worship could be of any faith. Only two conditions were given. They had to be a minimum of one hundred years old, qualifying as a heritage building, and they had to be functioning places of worship and not empty monuments. An e-mail contact was created for the responses. So was a post box address.

The response was overwhelming. The number of e-mails, post cards and letters was nothing short of a deluge.

⌘ ⌘ ⌘ ⌘ ⌘

To tell you the truth, some of us were worried about where this was heading. Yes, I was one of them. I admired the JM group, I often wished I had some of their gumption, the spunk, but I somehow could not get myself to be part of the enterprise. Did I quit? No, that is not correct. I never joined. Do you see the difference?

I can't expect you to. You are doing your job, you will see what you want to see. I am one of those who feel strongly about some things, but can't get down to doing things. I realized that I am not alone. There are many many like me. Even among the great sea of admirers of Shukria. Not many will act. I asked the group, "If you get into trouble tomorrow, what do you think your sea of admirers will do? Will there be a tidal wave of protest through the streets in your support?" The group was completely agreed that the readership would do nothing. They were surprisingly blunt in saying that they should expect nothing. I will say this. My admiration for JM went up further. So did my anxiety. I was worried for them. I wished there was some way to stop them before they got into some trouble, before they got hurt.

⌘ ⌘ ⌘ ⌘ ⌘

Meanwhile, the Group was working furiously on the follow up essay. It was titled Cleanliness-Godliness. Eddie, GK and Tina had developed a hygiene index for public places. Once again, a set of critical parameters fed into the index. It included innovative measures of litter in the premises, mapping the spitting, estimating the density of flies, the disposal of food waste, the cleanliness in the kitchen, the level of contamination in the drinking water and the state of toilets, as well as the ratio of toilet use to use of spaces within a radius of fifty meters from the shrine for either form of excretion.

Tina was tracking the responses of readers and working towards a three dimensional taxonomy of the places of worship based on geographical location, faith and denomination, and volume of attendance. The spikes in attendance on special festive occasions was brought into the computation. The readership response gave Shukria the confidence to attempt something new.

The next essay was a non-essay. It simply fed back the response pattern to the readership. It was revealing. There was indeed a pattern emerging and agreement on the most important religious centres to represent Indian heritage.

⌘ ⌘ ⌘ ⌘ ⌘

Tina's mother left a message on her cell phone. "Tried calling Pl call bk Urgent". She saw the message when the group took a break from the brainstorm session. Cell phones were strictly taboo in these sessions. They were put on silent mode and left on Noshir-kaka's desk. Tina called her mother. She was distraught and had a long story to tell. She was leaping wildly from one point to another. She was sobbing. Tina took some time to calm her and get her to start at the beginning. And to go strictly from one moment to the next in what she wanted to tell her. There was more sobbing, and finally she began. Ravi uncle had called on the land line when she was away veggie shopping. He had left a message on the recorder. "Call back as soon as you can. This is urgent. Tina and her friends are in danger. I must talk to you." Ravi uncle was calling from the

Club. He was with his drinking buddies, which included Mr. Mishra, the Joint Secretary in the Home Ministry.

The minister himself had issued the order for action. It was to be communicated to the IG of Police over telephone. It was only a matter of two hours for the written order to reach the Commissioner of Police through the IG's office and the arrest warrant for all six in the JM group would be issued. The Commissioner, Mr. AK Sinha, who read, wrote and spoke Kannada more fluently than many in the IAS cadre, the no nonsense police officer who was revered by the force, had dared to ask his superior under what provision he should issue the arrest order. He was told bluntly, "Use your brains". Disturbing the peace, that would work. It had certainly disturbed the peace in the Home Ministry. The fact that the public loved the essay was inconsequential. Everybody was talking about religion and morality in India. The public had hit upon a Wah moment. There was even a demand that Shukria should go on TV.

It was only the Vande Mataram Sangathan who could not swallow the saliva of truth. This was the party within the party that had a say in all matters of cultural policy. Naturally, that included what was good education and correct history. VMS made the demands on the Honourable Minister to rein in Shukria. They also swamped the education and culture ministries. Ravi uncle had slipped out and made the call from the Gents wash room.

Tina rushed back to the brainstorm table to report the news. Too late. They heard the sound of sirens from two police vehicles and the screech of brakes as they stopped at the entrance downstairs. Within seconds there were heavy booted steps on the staircase. And then the heavy fisted knocks on the door. It was Thambi who said "No panic. Don't do anything rash, anything foolish." He walked across, opened the door, and greeted the police party. "Good evening. Can we help you?"

They were packed off without so much as a reciprocal good evening. That was Venky's mumbled observation. A2 mumbled in response, as they stumbled down the stairs, "What do you think? Is this a B-grade movie script?" Thambi continued in his deadpan manner, "Did anybody remember to switch off before leaving?" Eddie told the caretaker that he could lock up, and added in a whisper that he call Noshir-kaka and inform him about their abrupt departure.

⌘ ⌘ ⌘ ⌘ ⌘

All six were driven first to the Commissioner's office, where the charge was read out to them. It was a non-bailable warrant. They would remain in judicial custody until further orders. They would be lodged in two different Police Stations.

"Orders from...?" Venky dared to ask. The Commissioner said he was not obliged to answer the question. It was Thambi's turn. What was the offence? What had they done? The Commissioner picked up a sheaf from his desk and waved it under Thambi's nose. It was from Sanjay nagar Police Station. It reported rioting, arson, homicidal attacks and destruction of public property. The Reserve Police had to be pressed into service and tear gas shells lobbed to disperse the crowds. A 24-hour curfew had been imposed.

"And you dare to ask what is the offence", thundered the Commissioner. "You could be charged with inciting communal violence. Do you know where that can land you?" Thank your stars the charge does not mention communal violence.

The Commissioner's outburst drowned the beep inside Eddie's pocket. He took out the phone furtively to catch the message in caps: ON WAY GETTING BAIL STALL FOR TIME. He showed it to Tina. She counted ten and swung into action. Placing her hand on Eddie's shoulder she sank to the floor, and half dragged down Eddie himself. The others made space for her. A2 went down on her knees to loosen her clothing. GK pronounced in an expert tone that she was dehydrated. The Commissioner snapped orders for drinking water. He lent GK and A2 a hand to lift Tina's limp body on to a couch in the room. GK took charge and ordered the people crowding the couch to step back and give her fresh air.

A policeman arrived with a jug of water and a steel tumbler. He brought a woman sub-inspector with him who was an acknowledged expert in first aid. Not allowing her to display her skills, A2 asked her to help in simply dabbing Tina's forehead, neck and arms with hankies damped with the water. The woman sub-inspector suggested that they shift Tina to the first aid room, so that she could be examined more fully. A2 looked up at Eddie and GK for their opinion. The phone on the Commissioner's desk rang. He picked it up, listened for a moment and said, "Let them in". The door to the Commissioner's chamber opened to let in Noshir-kaka and Mr. Jaishanker.

Who did not know Jaishanker? He was the foremost criminal lawyer in Bangalore and an advocate in the High Court. They had just applied for bail for all six, and had come ahead to meet the group while the bail order was being prepared. Tina remained on the couch. With all eyes turned to the visitors momentarily, Tina coughed lightly to signal the start of her recovery. Two cushions were tucked under her neck, which seemed to help in her opening her eyes. "Water", whispered the sub-inspector with some authority, and Tina cooperated by sipping a few teaspoon-fuls. She was sitting up soon after. Everybody was relieved. Mr. Sinha knew Mr. Jaishanker well enough to admit that he was relieved too. Imagine this leaking to the media. He ordered for chai and got the group to sit around the conference table.

ꕤ ꕤ ꕤ ꕤ ꕤ

It was clearly a leak. The Post admitted that the essay had the go-ahead for inclusion in the Sunday edition. The two-pager tabloid distributed on Saturday afternoon all over Sanjay nagar was a complete surprise and a great shock. It had the essay in full and a long commentary from the VMS damning the conclusions in the essay. While the rioting and arson was on, a huge crowd had gathered in front of The National Post, shouting slogans and demanding the heads of the Management and entire editorial staff. Sensing trouble early, the Commissioner's office had posted a protection force in front of the newspaper office.

Mr. Sinha had only two questions. First, he wanted to know if the essay distributed was in fact what the JM group had written. He produced a copy of the tabloid distributed in Sanjay nagar. The group read it carefully and admitted that it was indeed their essay.

"That goes against you", said the Commissioner.

"Why?" asked Mr. Jaishanker. "What makes writing the essay a criminal act?"

"It offends the sentiments of a large section of the population."

"Does it?"

"Does it not? It amounts to saying that Hindus are filthy."

With great calm and patience Mr. Jaishanker explained that the essay simply placed data before the readers. It was entirely up to them to conclude what they wished to from the data. Mosques, churches, Jain temples and Sufi shrines were on the whole spotlessly clean. Hindu temples were woefully filthy. It was not an opinion. Their scores were deplorable on all the measures that went into the Hygiene Index. Nowhere in the essay was there a conclusion that "Hindus are filthy". The essay reported a survey that was simply a mirror. If some were not prepared to face the ugly warts they did not have to smash the mirror on the floor.

"All very well", said Mr. Sinha, almost agreeing, "but you also have the fact of a provocation disturbing the peace. The rioting and arson. I have to go by the book I am given."

"But do you agree that there is not a line in the essay that can be interpreted as a conclusion? You have to give this group credit for its maturity."

"That goes in their favour", agreed Mr. Sinha.

Mr. Jaishanker excused himself to make a call. He wished to know the progress on the bail order. He stepped outside to complete the call. In a change of tone the Commissioner asked Noshir-kaka and the JM group if they would like some more chai. He recommended the khara biscuit from the bakery next door. Noshir-kaka and Eddie wondered why the attacks took place in Sanjay nagar. It was such a liberal, cosmopolitan locality. That is where Shukria had the greatest fan following. Without looking up from his chai Mr. Sinha suggested, "Maybe that is the reason... Some people elsewhere are intolerant of tolerance."

When Mr. Jaishanker returned he was cursing under his breath. The bail had been denied. "Orders from above". The group would be held in custody after all.

Meanwhile, under great pressure and concerned with the security of its staff, The National Post issued a short editorial statement that the essay by Shukria scheduled in the Sunday edition had been put on hold indefinitely. There was no explanation, nor was any apology given. However, the editorial condemned the fact that unscrupulous elements had hacked computers and stolen the essay to use it for nefarious ends, leading to most unfortunate outcomes. The case was referred to the Cybercrimes Department. It was initiated by the Commissioner himself.

Mr. AK Sinha, IPS, returned home late. Mrs. Sinha was dressed to go out. She reminded her husband that it was Saturday. The Sinhas went to the Hanuman temple every Saturday evening. It was late, but they could still make it. Mr. Sinha tossed his briefcase on the sofa and went up to his wife to give her a long, warm embrace. She knew he had some other plan on his mind.

"Why not the Sufi dargah off the Bellary highway?"

"Dargah? On a Saturday evening?"

"It will be quieter. It will be much cleaner."

The Crossing

The noise was unbearable. Only those who know migraine know what truly unbearable noise is. As if the unending line of hawkers in the aisle was not enough, peddling tea, coffee, bread-omelette, veg-cutlet, hot vadai, hot idli, cool drinks and pirated music CDs with the music blaring from cheap loudspeakers, there was the family of six assembled on the lower berth, opening the khana dabbas. They were reliving the incidents at the wedding, punctuated by dey-taalis and cannon fire guffaws of the barrel chested man who seemed to be the head of the family. In the adjoining bay on the left was a high-decibel quarrel between two groups about who had the rights to the luggage rack between berths. No sooner had the matter been settled they broke into another argument about keeping the window open or closed. It was clear that these were just the beginning of many more quarrels to be fought though the journey. Then there was the sound of the bhajan from the right, complete with dholak, tambourine and lusty clapping. It was made even more unbearable by half the voices singing off key and the other half yelling along faithfully. And the sound of iron wheels on iron rails from underneath lent a demonic accompaniment to the pounding in his head. The steady shadagadum-shadagadum alternating with the heavier barrage when the rails merged and separated was more than merely agonizing. In fact at that moment Guru wished he could simply switch off all systems in his head, release the residue static out of his ears and let the world all around come to a halt. All silent, all dark. He thought it might work if he wrapped the entire length of the railway supply sheet tightly around his head and curl himself into a ball with the pillow clung over his face. He did that.

Guru awoke to a stillness he had not known before. There seemed to be light outside, but the stillness... it was as if he had pressed the mute switch on the remote. He could see things, but there was no sound. The small fan above within the grill was running. No sound. The information processing section of his brain had booted up, and he found himself seeking a label for the experience of silence. Eerie? It appeared too trite. A deathly silence? Funeral silence? Warm, but not quite there. The hard disk inside his head was racing through millions of synaptic connections to seek out labels. By the time he sat up two words had dropped on to the base of his tongue for consideration. Vast. Expansive. As he let himself down from the upper berth the vastness of the silence was fully established. He did not hear his own footsteps. Nor the thud of the shoes when he dropped them in front of himself. And then the expansiveness. It spread way beyond his bay, all along the corridor, well beyond the train itself. No sound.

Guru saw then that the train was empty. No passengers, no luggage, not even the litter and scraps of wrappers he remembered in the passage the previous night before he climbed to his upper berth. The entire compartment was clear. He reached into his pocket to take out a cigarette and matches. The match striking the side of the box and catching fire were both noiseless. As he leaned forward to light the cigarette he saw a single shoe in a corner under the lower berth. It was small, about the size his teen aged niece would wear. Or his petite aunt. It was a slip-on. It seemed to have a fabric upper, soft, with a thin, flexible sole. The fabric was black. It had tiny white dots all over it, and a bow on top, also of the same fabric, black with white dots. It seemed to be sharing Guru's bewilderment, being left alone in the compartment. Guru thought the slip-on was trying to say something to him, wanting to tell him its story, perhaps, or simply seeking his company in the rest of the journey to god knows where, taking god knows how long.

Guru put the match box away slowly, quietly, keeping an eye on the slip-on all the time. With the cigarette still held in his lips he reached out to the slip-on, very slowly, as if rescuing a frightened pup that had fallen into a ditch. He picked it up gently, not knowing the nature of injury and where it hurt, held it in the palms of both hands, and then transferred it to his lap. Not finding a rag or a scrap of newspaper around as one always would he reached into his pocket for his hanky. He stroked the slip-on to remove the dust settled on its coat. It looked brighter immediately. He let it lie on his lap undisturbed and finished his cigarette, unhurriedly, gazing at it all the while. He thought he saw it closing its eyes and cozying itself in the valley of his crotch. When the cigarette was spent he shifted the slip-on gently to the seat and reached the window to toss the butt out. Modern train compartments did not have ash trays. He also wished to find out where the train had halted. When he pushed up the window all he could see was an expanse of water as far as the eye could see in any direction. Was it a lake? A wide river? The water was resting absolutely still, bright blue, as if mirroring the bright blue sky above in obedience. He wondered if the land had been inundated by a flood while he was asleep, all the passengers evacuated by army helicopters. He rushed to the opposite side and slid open another window to peep out. All he saw was an expanse of desert, the sand dunes making magical patterns and shifting gently as if to a silent beat struck by the sun above. But no sound. Neither on the left in the water, nor on the right. Guru sat for a while, his hand gently placed on the resting slip-on. He decided he had to find out more. Stretching his hanky over the slip-on, leaving just the tip exposed, he ventured toward the door. It would be safer to open the one on the desert side, he thought, and tugged at the door. He heard the familiar grunt of heavy steel in his head, but not in his ears. As the door opened there was a gust of wind bringing in a layer of sand on the entrance floor. It was a cold blast. When he stepped out the bitter cold hit him at once. He reached instinctively for the long handle along the door frame to heave himself back into the compartment. On second thought he decided to brave the cold and walk to the front end of the train to size up the situation better. He walked past six, eight, twelve bogies and then realized that he could not see the front at all. The line of bogies was unending. He turned around and it was the same in the rear direction. A line of railway bogies stretched from one infinity to another infinity with an infinite expanse of desert on one side. He was sure it was an infinite expanse of water on the other side. Guru got into his compartment, closed the door and sat down. He closed his eyes and practiced the deep breathing his yoga teacher had taught him. He felt secure with the slip-on next to him.

⌘ ⌘ ⌘ ⌘ ⌘

When Guru opened his eyes he saw that the slip-on was on his lap again, the hanky still covering it and his hand resting by its side. A flood of warmth overtook Guru. He stroked the slip-on gently. There was an enveloping sadness too. He felt true sadness for the lost slip-on. At that moment all he wanted to do was to help it find its home, its parent, its sibling. What could he do? He looked left at the expanse of water, still there, and then right at the expanse of sand. The first decision was clear. He had to leave the train compartment. He had to take the slip-on with him. Should he venture into the water or should he take to the sand? He looked left and right once more, hoping for a miraculous sign to guide him, perhaps a floating twig, a wafting feather, a reflected message on the water, letters formed on the sand. Everything remained as still as before. He looked at the slip-on. That warmth again. This time he saw a beady spot of blue at the toe. The bead soon turned into a thin beam of light, as in his Nokia phone. It grew stronger by the second until it was a powerful beam of blue light aimed between his two eyes. It felt as if it was going right through his head. He could see nothing else. The entire compartment and all that was outside on the left and the right were shut out. All he could see was the laser sharp thin blue beam of light of immense brightness. It held for hardly a few moments before its retreat. As quickly as it had appeared the beam had now turned back into the bead on the toe of the slip-on. And then it disappeared. It was the black fabric with the tiny white dots again. Guru had found the sign he was seeking. It was the art instructor in school reminding him that the key to great achievements was not in signs out there, but in oneself. He chose the desert.

Guru picked up the slip-on, still wrapped in the hanky and put it into the left side pocket of his denim shirt, close to his heart. He pulled up his socks, checked the shoelaces, slipped on the jerkin he had rolled into a pillow, slung the rucksack over his back and walked to the door. He took one last look at the empty seats and corridor and opened the door to the right. That cold blast again. He stepped out quickly. He left the door open, just in case...

Standing with his back to the train compartment Guru bent his head for a moment to decide which direction to take in his expedition. He saw a patch of clear ground opening up before him. He stepped into the patch cautiously, only to see more space opening up ahead. With every step taken there were longer and longer patches appearing before him. Soon there was a stretch ahead that was clearly a path opening up for him. He began to walk with greater speed, greater confidence. If he happened to turn ever so slightly to the left or to the right, the path, too, changed direction to the left or right. It amused Guru. He tried playing with the sand dunes ahead, changing direction every few steps, and delighting in the obedience of the path before him. It was not without some anxiety. What if he turned around fully, even accidentally? Would he not be plunged into the expanse of water behind him? Guru decided to play safe and steer himself through a straight path directly perpendicular to the train. When he looked back, without turning around, he saw that the space left behind had filled up with sand again. He did not know how deep the sand might be. He did not think he should try to find out. It was best to walk straight ahead, he thought. Something was working. Why take a chance and lose it?

Guru had soon walked far enough to think he would be able to see the whole length of the train. He was curious how the water and the sand might be separated beyond the front end of the train. Or its rear. He paused, took a few sips of water from the mineral water bottle nestled in his ruck sack, and turned around. He could see neither the front end of the train nor the last bogie. The train seemed to have grown longer. He could not see the water on the other side of the train. He tried walking backwards, away from the train in the distance, only to see the train getting longer as he moved away from it. Guru realized that he had to put all thoughts of the water body aside, behind him really, and concentrate on finding a way out through the body of sand he had chosen. He trudged on, more determined now, and more methodical in his strides. It made the path opening up before him just that much longer and wider.

As he walked on, Guru realized he did not know how far he had walked. Or for how long. There was no sun above, just lots of light all around. It was not getting brighter or darker. The hands of his watch had frozen at 12 o'clock. Was it 12 noon? Or 12 midnight? He thought he would get some idea of the distance covered by looking at the train behind. It was still there, even longer than before, stretched all the way left and right. It did not tell him the distance. It did not tell him the time spent. There seemed to be nothing else to do but to keep walking. He was surprised that he did not feel any fatigue. Not knowing how long the light might last he struck a quicker pace. The path opened up ahead to a greater distance.

Way ahead, almost at the horizon, Guru saw what appeared to be small dots lined on both sides of the path. The path itself seemed to end there. He picked up speed, in some way sensing that journey was nearing its end. The dots grew bigger as he approached them. Soon he saw that they were indeed placed on the ground on either side of the path, but were irregular shaped rock-like figures, in different sizes and different shades of brown and grey. As he drew nearer their features became gradually clearer. They were human figures, lined on two sides of the path, packed close to each other. They were seated on their haunches, covered in sheets, shawls and blankets. They were staring in Guru's direction, unblinking, expressionless, motionless. When he was close enough he saw that they were all his fellow passengers in the train, from his compartment and the other compartments in the neighbouring bogies. The feasting family, the quarreling parties, the bhajan group, they were all there, huddled on the ground, on two sides of the path. Silent, motionless. Staring. Ahead, where the path seemed to end, there was a railway crossing barrier with freshly painted black and white bands, lowered to stop traffic. Guru dropped his pace. Taking one cautious step after another he reached the two lines of frozen passengers. He passed them, expecting them to make some move or say something as he did. They remained motionless, silent. They remained staring.

He finally reached the cross bar blocking the path. It was then that he saw the girl on the other side trying to catch his attention. She was waving at him, and trying to say something. She could have been in high school. Or junior college. About the age of his teen-aged niece. She was pretty and her smile was fetching. She was in an ankle length flowing skirt with a white embroidered shirt above and a plaited belt loosely tied over it. She wore a pair of silver anklets. The bare feet were the prettiest he had ever seen. He found it difficult to take his eyes off them. There was a string of polished stone beads around her neck with a matching bracelet on one wrist. Two silver earrings on both ears. Guru thought he could hear the anklets jingle as she kept shifting her weight between her two feet, but of course the sound was only in his head. She had a smart shoulder bag of handloom fabric slung across. Her cheery gestures were kept locked in the all-pervading silence. Guru heard nothing. He tried to lip read and guess what she was trying to say. It did not work. Finally he decided to take a chance and go across the bar, even if it was clearly down and not meant to be crossed. He tried at first to lift the barrier. It would not move. He then decided to crawl under it. As he stuck his head under the bar he heard the thundering sound of a train passing a railway crossing. The further forward he moved his head the louder the sound of the moving train became. He moved his head back a few times to test the sound. Louder and softer, it changed with the extent to which his body had crossed the bar. He was relieved at first to know that he had not lost his hearing. It was not a silent world anymore. By the time his chest had emerged on the other side the sound was as deafening as it was frightening.

Guru decided, with much sadness, that he had to stay on his side of the bar. He simply could not get to the other side. As he raised himself and stepped back he saw that the girl was downcast. There was a tear dropping from one of her eyes, followed by another from the other. There was something more in that expression. It was not clear if she was disappointed with Guru or angry with him. The tears stopped, as if in response to an inner command. Guru tried to speak to her and explain his predicament. Although he could hear his thoughts there were no words spoken. He hoped she would understand. Would she give him some sign that she had? The girl's expression changed, very slowly, and with a look of forgiveness accompanying it. Finally, she was smiling again. It was a quieter and mellower smile now. She reached into her shoulder bag and pulled out a single slip-on shoe and held it up for Guru to see. The fabric was black. It had tiny white dots all over it, and a bow on top, also of the same fabric, black with white dots. A blue coloured bead appeared on the toe. It began to turn into a thin beam of light. He felt a tremor in the left side of his chest. The beam grew into a powerful shaft of blue light aimed between his two eyes. It was soon a blinding white light enveloping his entire body. He could see nothing, feel nothing. And then the black out.

Guru came to his senses with the tremor on the left side of his chest still there, now slowed to gentler beat. Rather like a child sobbing. He put his hand over the pocket. The slip-on was still there, wrapped in the hanky. He opened his eyes to see himself walking. In front of him at a great distance was a long thick line stretched from the left to the right as far as he could see. He walked on, unmindful of time and distance. The long thick line was turning into a train with an endless line of bogies. No beginning, no end in sight. He picked up speed. He walked on.

The Confession

Dominic! He heard the familiar, raspy-soft voice of Father Rebello at the end of the corridor. He would walk up personally to greet every person, young or old, well-heeled or ragged. The same smile, the same handshake, warm, gentle, reassuring. The wooden flooring went silent every time he walked up, but resonated accurately the footsteps of every visitor walking down to his cubicle. Dominic tried to stay in step as the good Father accompanied him back, but there was only one set of footsteps heard. The degree in biology had made Dominic a keen observer of the way people used their bodies. He had noted long ago that Father Rebello's light steps had the backing of a sinewy carriage. Not many knew of his place in the University soccer team years ago.

When was the last time Dominic met Father Rebello for a confession? Three months ago? Four? Perhaps under a year ago. What was the right number of confessions in a year? Dominic had wondered about that over many years. Being a regular meant he was a faithful member of the church. It also meant being a regular. Not going there for a long time meant not seeing Father Rebello. The handshake was missed.

When was the first time? That was easy to remember. It was twelve years ago, a day after he was eight years old. It was a Monday. On the previous evening, after all the guests at the birthday party had left, Dominic had called his older brother a name that was, to say the least, unacceptable in the Benjamin family. It had to do with the dorsal-posterior section of his brother's anatomy. The effect had been electric. First, a moment of stunned silence, with every one of the five other persons in the room looking at one another, then at Dominic, then at one another again, in what looked like short bursts of an accelerated neck exercise. Putting aside any suspicion that continued silence might be the order of the evening, his mother fired the opening salvo with an extended high pitched shriek. Taking the cue, his father first produced a mandatory roar and then ran out of the room for no more than ten seconds, returning with the eighteen-inch ruler from Dominic's own arts class satchel. Twelve years later Dominic still smiled to himself when he remembered that moment, a high resolution image fixed in the front most part of his brain. He also remembered the exact feeling at that moment. He had caught a first glimpse of manhood, finding a voice, growing out of Hans Christian Andersen. He was confused too. At that very moment why was he so sorry that he had hurt his brother? And frightened? Not at being punished by his parents, but losing them. He had never before experienced such a strange and overpowering mix of emotions, all in the same moment.

Holding the ruler under his nose, Dominic's father asked him The Question:

"So, are you feeling good about what you just did?" Silence.

"Well?!"

The mist cleared, and Dominic had the answer. "Yes, father."

He was only doing what his parents always wanted him to do, to be truthful.

Another roar, and the left hand seized Dominic's shirt collar, even as the right hand kept the ruler under his nose. Just as he was lifted off the ground, to be taken in all probability to the garage for the straightening up ceremony, Dominic could not help wondering if there really was something like a miracle. Of course, there was. It was his mother. She moved in quickly, recovered by now, and took the ruler away from the father's hand. Dominic thought he saw a momentary sense of relief on his father's face, although the grip on the collar only got tighter. His mother spoke little in the Benjamin home, but when she did, it was understood that everybody must pay attention.

"It is sad. He knows not what he does. But he speaks the truth."

She said other things. So did the father. So did the others in the room, including Rita, the live in maid, who enjoyed the privilege of expressing her opinion whenever called for, and often when not called for. And thus it was agreed upon that the Benjamin family would adopt the following course of action:

First and foremost, Dominic would tender an unconditional apology to his older brother. This would be followed by an apology to all else in the room, as well as Mother Mary on the chest of drawers.

The brother would accept the apology and shake Dominic's hand. It brought tears to the eyes of all present, but was not to be talked about.

The father would put back the ruler in Dominic's satchel.

On the following morning, Dominic and his father would visit Father Rebello and have a little chat.

The family would not let the incident upset them, and certainly not talk about it to anybody else.

⁂ ⁂ ⁂ ⁂ ⁂

Dominic knew what Father Rebello's first words would be. He would make kind enquiries. He would look directly at Dominic, smile broadly, and ask, half singing, about "how are we keeping aaj kal...?" and "what are we up to aaj kal...?" As always, it was with great sincerity. He was all there, listening, tuned in. The enquiries were never a routine prelude to the main business of the meeting. It was so with all visitors, not for Dominic alone.

As always, he would allow Dominic to set the pace and begin with the business whenever he liked.

"Yes...?"

"I found myself..."

"Yes...?"

"I was alone...by myself..."

An understanding smile. A short pause. "Lonely?"

"Not exactly lonely, but all by myself..."

The smile held. "You did something you want to talk about..."

"Yes."

A longer pause, ever patient. "Whenever you wish to."

"I played..."

"By yourself?"

"Yes."

"With yourself?"

"You could say that."

There was the faintest hint of amusement in the smile.

"Eight years ago was the first time. Do you remember? I do."

"Father..."

"You are, what, twenty two now? We haven't talked about this in a very long time."

"Father, it's not that sort of..."

"I understand. What brings it on now can't be the same as what brought it on then."

"Father, it was the cell phone."

"Of course! There's a lot going around on cell phones nowadays. It's all so easy, it seems..."

The conversation went exactly as Dominic had imagined it would, to the exact same detail. In fact, he had written it down in a note book before starting out to meet Father Rebello that morning. He had even recorded his own feelings about the game he was going to play on the good Father. There would be a fleeting moment of guilt, but it would soon be overcome by the laughter and the warm embrace and the big hearted appreciation of a good joke, well carried. Dominic loved Father Rebello, and although it was never mentioned aloud, he knew he had his love in return.

Dominic took Father Rebello into his game as a team mate. He wished he could be made a business partner, but that was not to be. He explained everything to him in great detail.

Yes, he was indeed by himself when it happened, not exactly lonely, but all by himself and, yes, not quite himself. He wanted to reach out to somebody, but didn't know if such a person existed. He had the strange desire to – how should he put it – moan softly and to hear a voice in reply, equally soft, saying nothing more than a Hi. He took out his cell phone and opened his contacts page, looking at every one of the entries and imagining the face behind the name. He thought a one word sms might do: MOAN. One click, three clicks, one click, two clicks, send. Name, face, name, face, all the way from A to Y. There were no entries in Z. Not one of the faces behind the names seemed interested in looking at Dominic's sms. Disappointed, but continuing to play with the key pad unthinkingly, Dominic had created a fresh contact: Dominic Benjamin. He entered the ten-digit number. He sent Dominic Benjamin the sms: MOAN. In an instant his cell phone beeped. Pippety-pip-pip-pippety-peep. Dominic Benjamin had sent him an sms. What an intriguing message: MOAN. He could see the man before him, reaching out, waiting for him to reach out to him in return. He keyed in the message: HI. Send. Pippety-pip-pip-pippety-peep. Message delivered.

⌘ ⌘ ⌘ ⌘ ⌘

Father Rebello was not sure why Dominic had chosen this hour to meet him, and where this was heading. But he could not help being drawn in. He did not wish to interrupt Dominic as he described, not without some excitement, how he had, well, played with himself. He waited for Dominic to finish, which he did soon enough. Pause. Dominic grinned sideburn to sideburn, lovingly manicured over the years, and looked expectantly at Father Rebello, anticipating his half comic, half philosophical observation. Pause. No response. Father Rebello's thoughts had flown back eight years, and he had momentarily lost eye contact with the fourteen year old, now in a twenty-two year old body. Realizing that Dominic was silent and was in fact staring at him, he re-established contact. He cleared his throat.

"Very interesting...", he found himself saying, without quite knowing what it was.

"You really think so, Father?"

"Where did it take you?" That grin from Dominic again. "How far did it go?"

Dominic unzipped his ruck sack, and from an inner compartment with another zip he took out a blue tinted plastic folder. There seemed to be a collection of papers in the folder. He put the bag aside and kept the folder on his lap. Pause. Then, with a finesse that was clearly unrehearsed Dominic pulled out two separate sets of papers. The first had two sheets. The second was a single sheet. He held out the two sheets. They were un-stapled, but with the first page up.

"And this is...?"

"My first Twattle."

"What did you call it?"

"Twattle."

Father Rebello was not sure he had heard correctly. He asked again. Dominic was not the least surprised. He replied patiently that the world of Twattle was not known yet, but would be very soon. It had just been invented, and he wanted Father Rebello to be one of the first to know. Dominic then pulled out the single sheet and presented it to him with both hands, head bowed, as one holds a silver tray with a scroll before a person of eminence. It was a letter on company stationery from V-Tel, the country's third largest cell phone service provider operating in nine States, and all set to move into three more by year end. The letter commended Dominic on his innovative use of sms. It hailed the birth of Twattle as the most illustrious offspring of sms. As a suitable recognition of Dominic's inventive brilliance the company had announced an outright gift of fifty thousand rupees. Further, and this is what Dominic really wanted to talk about, the letter held out an offer of a contract by which the company would have exclusive rights to commercial usage of Dominic's intellectual property of Twattle, and offered a royalty for such use based on the extent of Twattle traffic over the mobile network.

Intellectual property in an sms? Father Rebello did not understand. Dominic explained that as soon as his friends had caught on to the game, and the friends of friends were getting on board fast, he had talked to Uncle Stephen and registered for a Trade Mark of the word Twattle, and a copyright on its usage.

"How does it work?"

"Simple. It gets people to Twattle more."

"You mean...send themselves an sms?"

"Not one sms. It has to be a complete twatten"

"A twat–ten?"

"That's right. A total of ten messages makes one twatten, five in one direction and five in the return direction."

"Not two or four, it has to be ten..."

"Not ten or twelve either".

Dominic explained that Twattle had become a new cell phone game. For people to take part there had to be some rules of the game. The five plus five messages was one such rule. There were other rules, about the length of the sms in any one go, the time within which all ten messages had to be sent, and so on. It was catching on faster than the flu.

Father Rebello now looked a bit worried. He scanned Dominic's face with the probing gaze of a seasoned counselor. He took some time to phrase what he had in his mind. He decided to make it The Question: "So... are you feeling good about what you did?"

Silence. Familiar words... but a very different tone. Dominic felt the warmth in the question. Father Rebello asked again, gently, patiently: "Well...?"

Dominic had the answer. "Of course, father."

Father Rebello's mind was racing, rummaging the archives, the training manuals, the notes from his internship, the counselor texts, the journals, the case studies, the seminars... It was back to the basics. When in doubt, revisit the problem definition. Most important, listen some more. He gathered himself quickly and started afresh.

"Would you like to tell me...what about the sms to yourself made you feel good?"

"It works!"

"Twattle works... In what way?"

"You can see it works because the Twats are growing by the hundreds everyday."

"Twats?"

"Those who are in Twattle. Twat is also a Trade Mark, owned by V-Tel."

There was a membership. There were weekly and monthly awards for the best Twattens. You could network with other Twats and share your Twattens. There was complete protection of your privacy, you could choose the Twats in your network. You made new friends through Twattle. Dominic could go on, but he waited for Father Rebello to say something. It was another question, good old Father.

"Why would anybody want to Twattle?"

"Like I said...."

"You have shown me that it is successful, not what it can do. Why be a Twat?"

"Better a Twat than a Twit."

"It doesn't answer the question. Why would anybody want to Twattle"

"It's fun."

Ahh, that was an angle worth looking into. Was it a sort of escapism? Could there be a dependency setting in? Father Rebello knew he was stepping into a whole new world. There was going to be a lot of new learning. He was glad that the person showing him around was Dominic. The boy was honest. And utterly true to himself, as always. He had not taken his eyes of Dominic's face as the preview of this journey unfolded before him. That grin again, those sideburns. Dominic glanced down and Father Rebello followed. There, on his lap, on the blue tinted folder was an envelope. Dominic slid it across to Father Rebello.

"What's this? Cash?"

"For the church Youth Club, Father. From me."

"There's so much in this..."

"Twenty five thousand. From me."

"Dominic, you really can't..."

The boy's arm was strong and firm. He pressed the envelope into Father Rebello's hands and held it there for a few moments, explaining why he had to accept the gift. It was clear Dominic was not a little boy anymore. Dominic announced that he had made up his mind to donate twenty percent of all his royalty earnings to father Rebello's Youth Club at the church. He had already worked out the standing orders with his bank account.

⌘ ⌘ ⌘ ⌘ ⌘

For two whole weeks there was no word from Father Rebello. He would get back, he had said. He wanted time, he had said.

When Dominic returned home it was already past dinner time. The family had waited till past eight and decided to go ahead without him. When he entered the dining area he saw that the meal had just concluded, but they were all still at the table, silent. All heads were turned towards the passage where Dominic stood, framed within the arch between the parted curtains. He smiled and waved his hand in greeting, but there was no response. The look on their faces turned from anxious to grave.

"Something wrong?" Silence. "I have some news." An indifferent silence.

"OK, I am sorry I am late, but I sent a message that I was delayed."

The family looked in the direction of Dominic's father. Pause. The father looked in the direction of the mother. The others hurriedly picked up their plates and left the room. It was left to his mother to open the conversation.

"Father Rebello was here, Dominic."

"Oh, I was expecting him to call."

"He came himself, said he wanted to see you personally. We asked if there was anything...anything we could do. No, no, he wanted to see you, he said." The parents exchanged glances and waited for a reaction from Dominic. Not finding one, the father completed the report.

"He waited till eight and left."

"Any message?"

"No. No message...Have you been up to some...?"

The telephone rang, saving both father and son the awkwardness of finding words to continue. The mother picked up the phone. It was him. She called Dominic.

"It's him."

"Father Rebello?" He took the phone. As the conversation with Father Rebello began he turned his back to his parents. Father and mother decided not to take the cue, and sat at one end of the dining table, their gaze fixed on Dominic, while he bent over the phone at the other end of the room. He spoke softly, but they picked up the key words and phrases.

"Sunday...your chamber...before service...nobody...strictly... no...yes..."

Dominic put the phone down slowly and remained bent over the stand. The father coughed and cleared his throat. Very slowly, and with noticeable effort, Dominic turned to face his parents. His face was drawn and his brow knitted.

Then, in the way the dark grey horizon at dawn turns bright orange over a whole minute, one inch at a time, Dominic's arms rose to his side, the palms opening upwards gently, in unison with the neck rising from its slump and the lines on his face smoothening out to a broad smile. The sideburns glowed.

⁂ ⁂ ⁂ ⁂ ⁂

At the Sunday mass, the attendance was unusually high. Posters pinned at various points in the church premises through the previous week had contained a gentle exhortation to members of the flock to spend more quality time together, more often. These were times of new and cunning diversions, rendering us all fragmented. We had to hold together, and confront the challenges with fresh vigour. Contributory coffee and snacks on Sundays were suggested.

Even as the receding echoes from the last hymn were lap dissolved with the sound of the congregation shuffling into their seats, Father Rebello rose to take his place at the lectern. There was a bounce in his step that had not been seen in over a year. It was clear to all who knew Father Rebello's many ways of taking to the lectern that this was going to be a sermon to stay awake. He chose his opening words very carefully, as always.

"Is it possible...is it just possible...that we have lost the art of talking to ourselves...and thus forgotten the immense benefit of attending to ourselves?"

It succeeded in securing the undivided attention of all in the congregation. The Benjamin family, especially, was all ears. Father Rebello took the long, measured pause that was known to signal the introduction of the main focus of the sermon. When he was sure the congregation had been adequately prepared he continued.

"Let me ask you today...and I beseech you to ponder over the question awhile before you leap to unhelpful conclusions... let me ask you...when was it last that you happily played with yourself?"

Is it in order for a congregation to clap at the end of a sermon? It was certainly the first time for Father Rebello. Outside, over coffee and snacks, there was a line being formed for fresh enrolments into the Youth Club. At the other end of the table, the newly elected Secretary was taking down names of donors and the amounts contributed to the Club. The cool shade of the verandah was inviting, with the red oxide floor below and the hundred-year old Mangalore tiles above. Many had moved there, taking Father Rebello with them. Seated in a circle that was growing in density by the minute, the good Father was coaxed into explaining the world-wide interest in the newly developed model of counseling by Twattle.

[An example of local innovation at the start of India's IT boom. The ecosystem was just developing. Not all youngsters had corporate desk jobs.]

•••

The Choice

What I wish to tell you is quite simple. When somebody says "we don't have a choice", it does not mean they see no choice. It usually means the choices are staring at them, But they don't know how to take the plunge. The longer they hesitate, the easier it gets to say that we have no choice. How do I know? I learned this from my father.

The story begins on the day my father sat me down at the small square table to teach me to play chess. I had watched him play with our Bengali neighbourhood friend many times. Uncle B, we called him, never able to pronounce his name correctly. Not easy even now. I had watched them so many times and for so long that I knew how to play chess without ever having played it once myself. It was the same with driving a car. I knew exactly what had to be done with the pedals and the gear shift to get started, pick up speed, take turnings, slow down and bring the car to a stop. When I was allowed to sit in the driver's seat the first time, which was on the day of my eighteenth birthday, my father was surprised at the ease with which I got going. I was not the least surprised.

Ah, but we were talking about chess with Father. Everybody in the family called him Father. I don't know how that came about. Ammaji was not called Mother. Everybody called her Ammaji. Father sat me down at the table and arranged the chessmen on two sides of the table, I knew he would place the blacks on his side, as he always did, playing with Uncle B. His very first words were: Chess is all about making choices. Before he finished I had taken the lead and made the first move. He looked up at me, shook his head left and right, and decided to hold back his advice till after he had won a round. He did, quite easily. He then continued: Chess is all about making choices. I found that fascinating. The options he had from my move, the options I had from each of the actions from his options, and so on. I won the second round. My father was strangely unmoved. It was as if he had expected me to win. He won the next three rounds.

At fourteen I won the chess Junior Championship at the state level. Father wanted to apply on my behalf for the Nationals eight months down the line. I wanted to say no. I was not sure I was ready for it. I had to train more, and I had to practice with tougher competition. Father insisted that I give it a shot. I did not know how to say all that was in my head. I struggled, it was at the tip of my tongue, but I could not say it. I found myself nodding. I practiced with father. He had a book open next to me when we played. We had a long analysis after each round. Post-mortem, he called it. I did not like the sound of the phrase. It gave me the smell of a hospital ward.

I went to the Nationals, determined to keep my head up and my spine straight. They collapsed when I was eliminated half way through the tournament. We did not speak much on the long train ride back home. After the thali meal arrived I picked up the courage to ask father if we really should continue with my chess. I heard his considered reply in my head before he spoke the words: "We don't have a choice." The train rolled on. The lights went out one by one. Father stretched out.

I sat looking out of the window. The sight of the engine at the head of a curved line of bogeys was like a scene from a Hindi film I had seen a month ago. When I was younger we made trains like that from empty match boxes. I tried to list the films in which there was a train shown hurtling against a moonlit night sky. I fell asleep seated at the window. Father woke me to announce that our station was ten minutes away. The lights in the compartment came on one by one. Father shuffled towards the toilet. I preferred to wait till we reached home. I gathered my bag from under his berth.

⌘ ⌘ ⌘ ⌘ ⌘

Dinner was served. I could see that my father wanted to continue longer at the chess table. He was not eager to go in for dinner. I thought I knew why.

Ammaji had a favourite topic for the dining table conversation. After serving the first round of hot chapatis to the two brothers and my younger sister and my father, she took her seat and began with the wish that we had a proper cook. She meant a maharaj, who knew a hundred recipes, but a woman who knew fifty would do. She took a long pause, chewing her first mouthful of roti-sabzi. We all knew what was to follow. But what she said this time was different.

"You really must find a way to get ahead in your job." Father's response was instant, trying to get the topic out of the way.

"My job? What's wrong with my job?"

"Your professional career." There was no response. Ammaji was not giving up. "At least your future in this job"

"We don't have a choice."

On that day it sounded different. I heard a sound I had not heard before. I had sensed that there were problems at his workplace, but he never talked about his work at home. It was a printing press. A weekly news magazine and a monthly journal of critical essays came out of the press. There were also the brochures, newsletters, letterheads, wedding invitations and the occasional book publication that kept up the cash flow. In recent times the press had been raided by the police, not once but twice. The investigations were spread over several weeks. Father returned home late, sometimes after midnight. What can I say about the family's anxiety, waiting in the front room? Quite predictably, he always entered upright and beaming.

The words echoed around the dining table.

"Your future in this job".

"We don't have a choice..."

My mind wandering took me immediately to a scene in Father's office.

I saw him stand in front of his superior's desk, head bowed, nodding now and then to show that he was following instructions. He did that a lot, head bowed, nodding left and right. He did not look once into the face of the boss. He knew every scratch and every stain on the desk, but he did not know the colour of the tie the boss was wearing. There were others in the room. They were seated. Some were on chairs behind the desk. There were others in chairs around a coffee table in the room. Father was the only one standing. He was nodding now and then.

I felt fingers running through my hair. I snapped out of the reverie and looked around. Dinner was over. The table was being cleared by Ammaji. Father was standing behind me, stroking my head. He asked softly, "Another few games before you go to bed?"

Ammaji stopped and stared at us. Father was looking down at me. He didn't notice.

"He could help me clear up first", she said with quiet authority. Father nodded in agreement and sat down at the table. Ammaji suggested that he should go and watch the news on TV. There was talk of a bundh being called. If it was true, she had to stock up milk and vegetables first thing in the morning. A bundh, wondered Father. In this day and age? Protests and processions were things of the past. Who would be able to gather even a hundred souls willing to be seen protesting publicly? I saw his head bowed, nodding left and right. Ammaji explained that it would take time. She was going to take my help in doing the dishes as well. Why me, asked Father. The younger one, Subhash, he should be helping out in house jobs too. Ammaji seemed prepared for the question. Subhash and Suhasini had enough to do. They could help out next year. Father understood. He saw at once that Ammaji had planned a talk with me in private. He left the room.

"Don't forget to feed the cat." Ammaji was simply making sure that father was out of earshot. I waited to be given instructions. Should I begin with the thalis?

"Sit down" was her reply. I obeyed. She picked up the thalis and piled them. She placed them in the kitchen sink, returned and picked up the dal and subzi dishes. I heard the whup of the fridge door. One more trip and the table was clear. She washed her hands, wiped them on her sari and stood before me on the other side of the table.

"Father has lost his job." She sat down. I expected to see her crying. She looked me hard in the face. After half a minute that lasted more than half an hour she spoke up.

"We must all act together." And after a pause, "We have responsibilities."

I did not see at that moment what responsibilities she had in mind, but I understood immediately what it meant to be the first born. The destinies of the second and the third were charted out even before the moments of birth. Remarkable milestones on the road were reserved for the unremarkable first born.

I had to take up a job. I shelved my plan to study for a diploma course in hardware manufacture and servicing. I was sure I could manage a part time job side by side with some form of online study course. Getting a job was the first priority. What sort of job? What sort of income could I expect? The bigger question was: who would give me a job? I didn't know anything except chess.

The reputation of Father's press seemed to help. I was approached by a senior journalist attached to a large newspaper chain. A meeting was arranged with the Editor himself. I was offered the position of a junior reporter, without having to go through the step of an unpaid internship. I would report to an old hand who would assign me work and also teach me the ropes. I wondered what beats would be assigned to me. I looked forward to covering the newsiest of news stories. I had heard that journalists got to see the underbelly of a city like nobody else did.

My assignment was going to be different. In the first month I was given some routine news reporting jobs. An inauguration here, a school annual day there, press conferences, interviews, festivals and the like. I soon realized how easy these jobs were. I did not have to be clever in reporting anything. I simply had to keep my eyes and ears open. And write sentences that were both correct and interesting. I sensed a fear surfacing that I would get bored with the job soon. I felt the need to have a chat with my mentor.

He was called Dada in the inner circle. He did not mind my calling him that. It did not mean I was part of the inner circle. I just felt warm under his wings. Dada took the lead and said I had passed the trial period of two months that he had set up for me. The story I had done on a dargah at the junction of a temple street and a Muslim mohalla had been particularly well received. What he really meant was that the story had not received any protests from the expected quarters. I was ready for a bigger assignment, with less supervision. Was I ready for it?

It was reporting of a different kind, he began explaining. What came out of it would not be something visible or make headlines.

It would be research into streams of life that make the city what it really is. If it succeeded the study may be extended to other cities and other parts of the country. I thought it sounded really interesting, even exciting, although I had not understood one bit of what he meant. Dada then gave me two books to read. There were over twenty references added. I had to do a lot of reading up before we met again. At that time he would give me a more detailed brief about my new assignment. As I rose to leave Dada said there were two important points to remember. First, I was free to change my mind and withdraw from the assignment.

Second, if I took it on, I would be sworn to secrecy about it. In fact I would not even be known anywhere as a reporter of this newspaper.

The books and the readings were all about the subject of indoctrination. How people's beliefs are changed. I had never imagined there was so much written about the subject. There were the twin goals of drawing people away from something there already and leading them to something else. There was political indoctrination, and there was religious indoctrination. It was all very scientific, drawing from so much in sociology, psychology, political science, history, and so on. There was an impressive case study of over fifty pages on how the political and religious indoctrination streams were combined in a massive programme covering an entire state in the country. It was intriguing. It was also frightening. There was also the fascinating research method in anthropology.

It was all about getting at inner truths by shedding the role of the investigator from the outside and becoming one with the community. I decided to tell Dada that I wanted an opportunity to try it out. He smiled and said that it was indeed my new assignment.

The brief. Dada organized a meeting for me with three others. They were introduced as members of a team spearheading a nation-wide research programme. I was to work on a project code-named "Plasma Refraction". I would be embedded in a community setting as a volunteer, helping in one of their ongoing social-cultural programmes. The team would arrange that for me. I would take part in all they did, and become one of the community. I had to listen keenly to all that was said and discussed, getting at what they really meant, engaging people in discussions, but without getting into debates. I would never ever ask prepared questions as in a newspaper investigation. I would spend about a month in each community setting, deciding on the exact duration on my own. I would move on to eight such embedded locations. The locations ranged from an upper class club to a community centre organized in a slum by an NGO. I would never be seen taking notes. Listening and remembering were my key challenges. I had to go to the hostel accommodation arranged and key in all my observations in a five-page format on a daily basis, post them on a cloud platform called Plasma Research and immediately delete the file from my laptop. I loved it.

I had to address three research questions listed on a slide projection. First, what do people really talk about, what do they say? In other words, is there a difference between what the newspapers, magazines and TV channels were reporting and what people themselves saw and really felt? Second, what do people really want as the good life? What do they dream of, long for? Third, what do people really feel about other faiths and religious practices in this country?

The brief lasted nearly three hours. The team members left, wishing me well in the assignment. Dada stayed back for a chat. Just before we closed, Dada asked if I knew what had happened at Father's workplace. Vaguely, I said. Could he tell me more?

He could, he said. We walked over to the park nearby. We found a bench tucked away in a cluster of trees. Dada came right to the point. The old management of the press had caved in. It had been building up for some time. The end came quickly. The old management caved in. They saw no choice. Father had to either go along or go out.

⌘ ⌘ ⌘ ⌘ ⌘

Parthanjaya Printers and Publishers, affectionately known as P-3, was over 55 years old. The printing press basked in its past reputation. There was much public adoration, which included good will in the trade. The commitment to integrity was backed by courage of conviction. The press had taken up printing contracts with publishers who got to be regarded by the government as, well, troublemakers. They had fearlessly published articles and essays exposing marauder acts by people in high office. In most cases the nexus with the government in power had been exposed. Police compliance was not improbable. The reactions of the readership were mixed. Many wrote to praise the fearless stand the publishers took. There were others who said it was not what they expected from the publications, and even discontinued their subscriptions. Other newspapers and magazines took up the subject of freedom of reporting, and even referred to the articles most quoted. That is as far as they went. They never dared to publish a similar story themselves.

The government was embarrassed, but was also helpless. On public platforms they swore to uphold the freedom of the media, invoking the sacredness of the Indian constitution. On one such occasion, the inauguration of a literary festival, the Home Minister and the Editor of the journal were on the same Panel. The closed door discussions in the Ministry were something else. Elimination was the word most used. At last an Assistant Commissioner came up with a masterstroke.

ACP Ashok Mehra, IPS, raised his hand. He was permitted to comment. What if the publications could not be seen? Stop the printing press, and you stop the publication. It took a few moments for the comment to sink in. Finally, the Minister exclaimed, "Brilliant!" He was clapping. The gathering around the rosewood table could not help join the clapping.

Parthanjaya Printers and Publishers. The name reflected the dharmic path adopted by the principal promotors, Parthasarathy and Dhananjaya. Their talents were naturally complementary. If you closed your eyes you saw them together on a chariot drawn by four horses. Started as a Limited Liability Partnership firm with two promoter-entrepreneurs, the press had a focus on graphics, stationery and bulk printing for educational institutions. The press had grown steadily in the last twenty five years. Diversification in operations came naturally. So did upgradations in print technology. The Management had opened its doors to infusion of funds when the last renovation and installation took place. That was about five years ago. The firm was restructured as a Private Limited Company. The Board was expanded to seven members. Mr. Parthasarathy stepped down from his hitherto informal leadership role, but continued on the Board. His co-promoter, who was also responsible for securing the funds and restructuring, stepped in as the new Chairman. An old time family friend came on board as an advisor. The four others were those who brought the funds in. One of them also represented the bank.

You can guess what happened then. In an earlier time, when investigations were engineered against the Partnership firm, there was nothing to fear, because there was nothing to hide. A strong and upright Chartered Accountant showed the promoters how to ward off the attacks, yet remain transparent. In the new dispensation the Board systematically introduced practices that were quite different, to say the least. They replaced the Chartered Accountant. The two promoters looked on helplessly as they were outvoted time and again in matters of crucial policy. The last straws were actually a pair of them in quick succession. First, the Board passed a resolution to accept printing contracts for a newsletter which was actually an arm of a political party. The argument was that the Press needed to demonstrate its neutrality. The hollowness of this stand was clear when the agenda for the following meeting was announced. The Press would stop printing the weekly magazine and the journal that had attracted so much controversy. It turned out soon enough that the family friend and advisor was part of the majority vote. He was, in fact, set up by the new Board members. The management caved in.

Dada asked if there was anything more I wished to know before he concluded. I could only mumble a half response. I suppose Father had meekly submitted to the Management ordinance, I said. There was...no choice? Dada shook his head. He spoke firmly. No, Father stood his ground, and defied the Board of Directors. As had a few old timers, including the sixty year old Chief Editor. The Board had found a solution for the Editor's obstinacy. They invoked the retirement age and gave him a farewell party. They did not know what to do with my father. They thought he was wise enough to understand. They offered him two options. First, a voluntary retirement package that gave him enough cushion till he found something else to do. The second was a change of job. He would be taken off the operational team. He was offered the position of Logistics-in-Charge. It was a critical role in the business, they told him. Father's reply was that the job was the same as a delivery clerk, whatever the fancy title now being given. The Board was emphatic. Take it or leave. He was given twenty four hours to decide. He took it.

Dada rose, put his arm around me. He spoke softly now. Father accepted the job. Oh, yes, it was humiliating. He accepted it because he had three children who had five more years of schooling ahead. He would find ways to supplement the income from his new job as Logistics-in-Chief. I realized only then that Father had been leaving early every day and returning only after we had all had our dinner. For two hours in the morning he was engaging a tuition class of twenty students, teaching them new math. In the evening he was running a chess coaching school.

⌘ ⌘ ⌘ ⌘ ⌘

Dada gave me a warm hug and walked away. He stopped to say that the following week had Independence Day on a Friday. I could take the long week-end off and spend quality time with the family. The hostel would be informed. My schedule for the next three months would be delivered to me by hand. A man in a dark brown kurta would meet me at the biriyani café next to the furniture shop on the service road.

My understanding of Dada's mission acquired a fresh meaning after our meeting in the park. The woods were indeed dark and deep. I felt a new pride in the task I had been entrusted. I held my head erect and hummed as I approached the biriyani café. The man in the brown kurta turned to face me. It was Father. I froze. He stepped forward and embraced me. I cried. He whispered in my ear. We have to keep going.

The Draw

Eyes down for the full house! "Ladies and gentlemen, the last house of the evening!"

Ratna Patanwala picked up a fresh pencil from the glass tumbler before her and placed her wrist on the table, at the ready.

"Here we go... Opening with... Half a century, five and zero, fifty!"

Five more calls and it was over. Two hands went up with whoops, and the winners shared the final prize amount of two thousand four hundred. There were cheers all round by the older members and some boisterous woo-hoos by the younger ones. Chairs were pushed back noisily and the members rose to end the evening with hugs, back slaps and air kisses.

"Thank you, ladies and gentlemen! We meet next month on the first Friday. Same time, same station! Enjoy the rest of the evening! The bar will be open another twenty five minutes, I believe. Order your refills right away. Good night!"

Ratna put her four pencils back into their case, zipped it up, put the case in her purse and rose to leave. She was dressed in her Friday best, as always. Her carriage was straight, unhurried and dignified. Always smiling, she radiated tranquility. If they ever had a beauty contest for senior citizens she would win hands down. The heads of the newcomers turned as she walked past the caller's table, wishing him good night. They wanted to know who she was.

"Aah, Mrs. Patanwala. Ratna Patanwala."

"Does she always come by herself to play Housie?"

“Always. She is here five minutes before start, and leaves immediately after we close.”

“A regular, huh?”

“Ever since I have been at the caller’s table That’s fifteen years now. They say she has been a regular even before that. Every single first Friday. And every special Housie evening without a miss.”

What the caller did not tell the youngsters was that Ratna Patanwala had never won a single Rupee in all the years she had played Housie. Not a single line done, no corners, no full house, of course, not even the first number off the mark. She came in every Friday, she took her favourite seat, facing West for good luck, she played her booklet of eight leaves and left. Always smiling. Not once had anybody heard as much as a sigh from her when she missed a win by one number. Other regulars left her seat at the table vacant, sure that she would turn up just before the start.

The staff kept an empty glass tumbler before her seat for the four pencils. She wore a peach coloured sari on Housie Fridays. It had silver embroidery that went well with the three strings of pearls around her neck. The contrast blouse had elbow length sleeves, crossing over to the top of her forearm. People who looked closely realized that it was not the same sari. She had a collection of embroidered peach coloured saris.

The brash new President of the club once asked Ratna why she continued to play Housie on Fridays when she had, you know... She replied with another question, punctuated with a smile, “Why do you wipe your nose with your palm when you start to speak?” Caught unprepared, the President said, “Oh, a habit, I suppose. I must do something about that.” Ratna replied, “We all have our habits, I suppose. I certainly don’t propose to do anything about this habit.”

⌘ ⌘ ⌘ ⌘ ⌘

Housie, Tambola, Lotto, the club pastime is known by different names. They say it might have originated in Europe. Perhaps Russia. The game appears in one of Chekhov's stories, does it not? Perhaps in Harappa. Ancient Indians had an advanced number system, did they not? Is there any club anywhere in India that doesn't have Housie? Even home kitty parties are assured high attendance if the announcement includes Housie. The prizes range from a single Rupee for the first line to ten thousand for the full house. Of course big time Housie has big ticket sales of playing booklets. Not all Housie prizes are in cash. One club in Calcutta that is credited with the invention of tin and bottle badminton tournaments also introduced a tin and bottle housie evening. Only once a year. The rest of the time it was hard cash.

Another habit of Ratna Patanwala was in the generous tips she left for the staff in all parts of the club. The staff adored her. It helped on rainy days. At least two of the staff would come running with two umbrellas to escort her to the car. Ratna drove a Hindustan Contessa. It was the first generation classic 1985 model that could be recognized anywhere in Bangalore because of its distinct two-tone paintwork of maroon and cream. It was also the only Contessa with a luggage carrier above. That was because Ratna was a social worker. The car was frequently ferrying all manner of supplies to all kinds of people in all parts of the city. The car had also made trips to Doddaballapur and Anekal.

Ratna's husband of forty years, Gaurang "Goru" Patanwala, accompanied her sometimes, seated on her left, but most times he rode a bicycle. Anything less than four miles was always on bicycle for him. Anything more than a quarter mile was always by car for Ratna. They counted in miles. Groceries were in kilos, but body weights were in pounds. At five feet five inches Goru was two inches shorter than Ratna. And about twenty pounds lighter. All his shirts were striped, mostly in blue-grey, but a few in other pastel shades as well. All his trousers had turn-up bottoms. He had one pair of black Oxford shoes that were meticulously cleaned and polished every day. They never revealed their age. His other pair was the canvas tennis shoes. His socks were either white or black. Nothing else and nothing in between.

Goru was never seen in the Housie hall. He played carrom and was in the carom room three days a week. He was the longest reigning club champion in carrom and was six times inter-club champion. His deadly opening strike with assured pocketing was carrom legend. There were games when the opponent took strike only two or three times. Goru Patanwala finished all his pocketing in two turns. Some young people would not take to carom because of him. There were others who waited till he left the room and then went in. Yet, his manner at the table was always gentle and humble. Many first-timers would see that as meekness. Goru sir would often coach his opponent during the game, even allowing a second or third try.

On the Fridays that Ratna went for Housie Goru took a bus ride to Shivajinagar. He loved to stroll around Russell Market, inside and outside. He found the sights and sounds and smells invigorating. Generally quiet most times, he switched off completely on these trips to Russell Market. He was not buying anything, so it did not matter. He submitted himself completely to all that was enveloping him. Towards the end of the trip he stopped at the kirana shop at the turn to the bus station. The shopkeeper smiled in recognition. Goru put up five fingers and took out fifty Rupees. The shopkeeper took out five lottery tickets, one of each colour series, and handed them over. Goru walked back to the bus stop and went home.

The draw was every Saturday evening. The winning numbers were out in the Sunday papers.

Nobody knew about Goru's lottery tickets, certainly none in the family and social circles of the Patanwalas. The two exceptions were Ratna and the live-in maid. Out of the five tickets bought one was for Mary-amma. On reaching home he shuffled the five lottery tickets, held them spread face down, and allowed Mary-amma to pick one. Ratna had no comment. To each his own, she always said. Goru had never won a single Rupee in the lottery. Not even a consolation prize for the last three digits.

Young people meeting the Patanwalas for the first time were amused by their differences. Chalk and cheese, they said. Oil and vinegar, poles apart, baigan and bhindi, that sort of thing. You have to be married at least thirty years to understand that it's the differences that make a great marriage. You think differently, act differently, but come into sync every now and then. That's jazz.

One day, on his way out of the club, Goru saw a middle aged person seated on his haunches by the side, attending to his old bicycle. He was a working class person, poor, emaciated, perhaps a daily wager or a hawker. There was a boy of about twelve helping him. Stopping his own bicycle Goru went up to the man to ask what had happened.

"Nothing, sir, it's all right."

"But you look like you are in some difficulty. Tell me what happened."

The man was indeed a daily wager, working for a construction contractor. He had stopped to put back the chain that had slipped. A lady driving out of the club had nudged the bicycle and he had fallen with it.

She had stopped the car, got out, and attended to the man. Seeing that he was not hurt and there was no damage to the bike she had driven away. Goru was not satisfied. The trouble with society women! They should be taught a lesson. If only the man had taken down the number of the car. The man was in no condition to think of such things. The boy piped up to say he did remember the number. Good! Goru persuaded the man and the boy to accompany him to the nearest police station. He left his own bicycle at the stand in the club. At the police station Goru helped the man lodge a complaint. It was entered as rash driving resulting in damage to the chain gear of the bicycle. Goru returned to the club, picked up his bicycle and pedalled home. He parked the bicycle in the verandah and entered the living room announcing his arrival.

"What took you so long?" Ratna spoke first.

"You'll never believe what happened on the road just outside the club", Goru began.

"And you'll never believe what happened here a few minutes ago", she replied. "A police inspector dropped in to investigate a case of rash driving. It was a lady driver in our car."

⌘ ⌘ ⌘ ⌘ ⌘

Friday the fifth. The word had spread in the Housie room. It was Ratna Patanwala's birthday. When she entered the hall, exactly five minutes before the first round, a hush descended on the gathering. Ratna stopped to see if something was wrong. Somebody stuck a chord on the piano in the corner. The entire gathering joined in singing Happy Birthday to dear Ratna Aunty. She thanked them and announced that she had arranged a cake. But it would appear only at the end. It was time to begin the first round.

A bearer helped Ratna put the pencils in the glass tumbler. He placed a glass of orange juice before her. She hadn't ordered one, she protested. On the house, he replied, and added that she could ask for more. "Good luck drink", the bearer winked and smiled. He hovered around the table to make himself useful. Round four and it was eyes down for the full house. Ratna lowered her reading glasses to peer into the leaf. Just one number remained to be crossed. The bearer moved to get her another glass of orange juice. He stopped briefly on the way at the caller's table and dusted a speck of dirt off the table. His white gloved hand lingered on the table just a second longer. When the bearer had left the room the caller announced, "Two hockey sticks... Seven and seven... Seventy seven!"

There was no response. A second later a young woman seated next to Ratna screamed, "Ratna Aunty, that's your number!" All eyes turned to the table. Finally, Ratna raised her hand, her head still bent over the leaf. A moment later she raised her head, an embarrassed smile on her face. She rose and walked over to the caller's table for the very first time with the filled leaf.

The crosses on the leaf were confirmed. The gala prize of four thousand Rupees was confirmed. The entire gathering converged on the caller's table to congratulate Ratna Patanwala. A minute later the cake was rolled in. The celebrations spilled over to the bar. Ratna allowed herself an extended stay and joined the group with a glass of sherry.

Goru returned from Russell market and decided to have an early dinner. Mary-amma had made a delicious pumpkin soup that could not wait till Ratna returned. At a half past ten he went to bed, the five lottery tickets still in his wallet. He would give Mary-amma her ticket the next morning. When Ratna returned and found him asleep she decided not to wake him. She would tell him about the Housie prize the next morning.

Breakfast on Saturday was late. The entire morning was spent discussing what they should do with the four thousand Rupees. By lunch they had made up their mind. They would present the amount to their precious Mary-amma. It was going to be Easter the next week anyway. Goru was given the job of announcing the gift. And, by the way, the lottery tickets were on the telephone table. She could pick up any one of them. She did, leaving the four others on the telephone table. That evening Mary-amma had a call from her son who worked as an apprentice in a fabrication workshop. He had received an urgent call from the kirana shop in Russell Market. One of the lottery tickets sold from his shop had won a prize of one lakh Rupees. Could it be among the five that Patanwala-saheb had picked up?

When Ratna and Goru returned from their dinner engagement that night they were surprised to see the lights on in their living room. As they drove in and stopped the front door opened and Mary-Amma posted herself at the doorway. She held out all the five lottery tickets from the telephone table, face down, and asked Goru sir to pick one.

The Launch

First there was Adi.

You know the story of Emperor Vikramaditya and the tramp who was invited to a feast in the palace? There! I have done it again, starting a story with the second person you. It was the second strictly no no we were taught in the creative writing class in junior college. The first no no was starting with the first person I. I think I have got over that one. But starting with a you has remained. Not every time I write, but every now and then. Anyway, you know this story? It was a cocky vagabond who thought the rich had no business to be rich, because they did no work at all except to sit on comfortable chairs all day and lie down on comfortable beds all night. Since the complaint was evidently directed at the Emperor, and it was often on the street outside the palace gate, and it was getting louder by the day, the wise Vikramaditya sent his Minister for Cultural Affairs to invite the tramp into the palace for a chat over a meal. Graciously thanking the tramp for accepting his invitation and seeking his permission to begin he ordered that lunch be served.

Wait, is this story really from the reign of Vikramaditya? Is it not from the Arabian one thousand and one nights? I knew that was coming. Every one of the mothers in the PTA group in school likes to show off her GK at these meetings. They think they are on a quiz show on TV. All we were doing was help the class teacher choose a play for the year end concert. No, not the Arabian Nights, it is an ancient Chinese tale. No, it is from King Solomon's times. Naturally, the debate began to heat up and the class teacher was no quiz master to enforce any order. So, what about the story of the baby and the two women claiming to be the mother? Where did that come from? The wise king asking that the baby be pulled in two directions by the two women? Didn't the jataka tales have the same things to say? People don't read the puranas any more. And so on. I had to step in, you see. Good sense prevailed. I also got them to see that in the current political climate it was best that Vikramaditya ruled.

So where were we? Yes, a servant carried what seemed a large silver basin while another held a pitcher over it, waiting for the Emperor to wash his hands. When he was done he asked the tramp to wash his hands too, which he did readily. The Emperor engaged the tramp in a lively discussion of economics, external affairs, art and culture through the meal, which began with hot and freshly puffed puris and mango pulp, followed by the creamy daal that the royal court was famous for all over the empire. There was a total of fifty six dishes. That's right, the chhappan bhog that the palace was famous for. There! I have done it again, ending a line with for. That should have been "the chhappan bhog for which the palace was famous". Anyway, the tramp could not decide which was more difficult, keeping up the conversation with the Emperor or doing justice to the fifty six dishes.

If you know this story you will also know that the dishes were not there at all, neither the food nor the serving vessels. They were all imagined, with the kitchen staff miming the service and the Emperor miming their ingestion, relishing each one of the dishes in a unique way. The tramp had no choice but to do the same throughout the meal. He knew better than to point out to the emperor that there was no food there. The story was heartily approved. Vikramaditya's Feast would be the play for the six year olds.

Well, there we were at the rehearsal in Adi's primary school. You know Adi! A born drama queen! She was to play the servant who brings in the pitcher of water. And other things to serve later. The class teacher was struggling with the boy playing the king, making little headway, when Adi steps in and shows him how to walk like a king, sit like a king, talk like a king. Everybody laughed. Except the boy's mother. The other mothers then suggested that Adi should play Emperor Vikramaditya. The boy's mother was astonished. Adi? A girl playing the king? Why not, chorused the others. It is a play, after all. For First Standard kids, after all. The teacher asked me what I thought. I saw from the corner of my eye that the boy's mother was all coiled up and about to throw herself on the floor and have a fit. I also saw that the mother of the boy playing the tramp was not present. Adi would be wasted in the part of the king. The real tamasha part in the play was that of the tramp. That's what Adi should play. And that's what Adi played. Is it all right to start a sentence with and? Anyway, Adi was a hit as the tramp.

They call her Diti in school. All her friends call her Diti. She is Adi at home. Do you know about the mistake? Have I told you? Our gynec said I was going to have a girl. I told her it wasn't important, and nobody in the family need know. I cried when I reached home and was by myself. I wanted a boy. I wanted to bring up a boy the way my mummy had brought up my younger brother. At the baby shower they asked if I had a wish. Wish? I said I knew it was going to be a boy. The date and time of his arrival were chosen to give him a first class horoscope. When they were ready to wheel me in I asked them to wait a minute and a half, so that the timing was perfect. When I was sufficiently awake in the ward a signal went out for the baby to be brought to me. The nurse whispered in my ear that I had a beautiful daughter. What did it matter at that time? I was ready to go back to sleep. I sensed some agitation in the room. Members of the family present there were sure there was some golmal and some switch had taken place between the surgery and the ward. I held the baby close and said "Look, she has Periyappa's learned forehead!" A girl in the family with the brains of the male line! That settled it. The text messages and e-mails were suitably edited to say a princess had arrived. Aditya gave way to Aditi. I slept another six hours.

One day somebody will write a book about Adi. About Adi and me. Bringing Up Adi. That would be a nice title. Maybe I will write the book myself. The second one came two years later. Two years of Adi, and I knew I wanted another girl. Which boy could ever match Adi? I would do an Adi Version 2.0. When I was sufficiently awake in the ward they brought me a baby boy. The family was jubilant. Mission accomplished! Aditya had arrived. Only, we couldn't call him Adi. No hurry, something would come up in good time. Maybe we'd call him It. When they left the room I cried a bit and went back to sleep. When I awoke it was there, right next to me, snug in its wrapping. That was good, I remember saying to myself. Boys can take care of themselves.

The day of the first dress rehearsal Adi was beginning to sound hoarse. The next day there was a fever as well. There was no point in taking her to our family doctor. He would order rest and rule out the concert. I took her to the local clinic next to the Xerox shop, where there is never a line longer than one, and ordered the MBBS to give her a shot of Irgapyrin (they don't make that anymore) twice a day, the next three days. He thanked me for the advice and complied immediately.

Adi was a hit as the tramp. I have already said that, haven't I? Her fever was gone and her voice was better, certainly good enough for a burst of thirty minutes on stage. Who cares what happens after that? But two hours before the show – I know I am starting a line with but – two hours before the curtain went up she had a head ache and was pukish. I stayed with her in the green room and backstage through the evening. I could see at least two mothers sniggering, but what do they know?

At the end of the show, when they were giving away prizes – Adi won the best actress prize, of course – the Headmistress made a special mention of Adi and her mother for their dedication to the play. The headache was gone. A beaming Adi received her prize and we went home singing "Side by Side" through the drive. When her father reached home she was fast asleep, clutching her prize.

⌘ ⌘ ⌘ ⌘ ⌘

Then there was Diti.

Myself Alok. From Kolkata. I have now learned to say 'Hi, I'm Alok'. I came here for college. I first got to know of Diti from Jas, a common friend. She kept talking about this turbo-charged classmate who had appeared in the City Times as the inter-collegiate Miss Creative of the year. Riding, modeling, poetry, pottery, trekking, Tanjore painting, lamp shade designing and vermiculture were a sampler of all that she had done in her nineteen long years. Not to mention being Secretary of the College Dramatics Club. I got to know her name was Aditi only from the City Times, which began by saying Aditi had been on stage since the age of six. That sounded familiar. My Mom liked to tell everybody that I was painting since I was five. It made me mad. I left the room whenever I saw it was coming. She was clever. She would ask me to serve the guests water and bring up the topic just when I had entered with the tray and glasses. She might as well have said I was on stage at the age of six months. That is when I won the Bonnie Baby prize in the Durga puja celebrations. We Bongs love bonnie babies. We Bongs love dramatics too. But this Bong loves to paint. And that includes stage scenery. I have remained bonnie all my life. Girls can't take their eyes off me. My waist line. They hardly look at my face. Jas does. She is different. She thinks I am cute – whatever that means. She thinks we were meant for each other. She hasn't the slightest anxiety in introducing me to friends like Diti.

Diti was going to play the lead in the annual college production. It was *Arms and the Man* by an ancient dramatist. He was a socialist, Jas said, trying to impress another Bong side in me, and asking if I would be part of the backstage team. I said why not, and went along.

I dropped in at a rehearsal after I was done at the studio. It was half way. I heard the commanding voice of a director as I approached the room, giving instructions with authority. I slipped in and sat in a corner. It was Diti. She was showing the wavy-haired actor playing the part of Captain Bluntschli how to stand, walk and speak as the Chocolate Soldier. Mrs. Iyer from the English Department, who I thought was the director of the play, was sitting on one side, script in hand, listening and watching with rapt attention.

Tea was served. Jas introduced me to them, first Diti and then Mrs. Iyer. Would I be nice enough to design the set and take care of the execution, Mrs. Iyer asked. Jas latched herself to my arm. I said yes. Diti took over. "Sit down. I will tell you exactly what I want..." Jas left us to talk to her friends on the cast.

I listened to Diti the next five minutes, my jaw dropping lower every minute. The tea got cold. She must have noticed that I had not spoken a word. She stopped and asked if I had followed. I asked in return who the author of the play was.

"Somebody called Shaw."

"Shaw...who? What's the full name?"

"Bertrand, I think. Mrs. Iyer will know."

"She chose the play for this production?"

"Nope. It was my mother."

I joined Mrs. Iyer in her corner and asked where I could get a copy of the play. She had a spare copy in her room, she said. I could pick it up the next morning. The full name was George Bernard Shaw, she informed me.

I had to find about more about Mr. Shaw before I picked up the script from Mrs. Iyer. I did. Mr. Shaw was clearly much more than a writer of pretty comedies. This play of 1894 had far more depth than chocolate cream. Imagine the war mongering and posturing and hypocrisies of military budgets today. How are modern armies any different? Think 1971. Think Wagah Border. *Wah Wagah!* That could be the title of a new script, but fully acknowledging the original work of Mr. George Bernard Shaw. If I could only get Mrs. Iyer to listen to me. And Diti. She didn't. They didn't. One was sweet and understanding, but couldn't help. The other was sweet and dismissive. The smile was exactly the same in City Times.

I didn't let that come in the way of my backstage work for *Arms and the Man*. Jas made sure of that. I started work on *Wah Wagah!* on the side. The gang at the studio pitched in. Four from the debating club came on board. They got a bunch from the contemporary dance and martial arts clubs to join. For the first time in the history of the college there were two productions of the same author, the same play actually, presented back to back over two week-ends. We didn't take a rupee from the college for the production. Not even the audi. Just permission to take it up and put it up. We performed outdoors. It was like a rock show. Yeah, we had music. Corporate sponsors and all. This Shaw guy, he was a genius. Five thousand people in the city got to know that over two nights.

It was opening night for *Arms and the Man*. The audi was nearly full. I was backstage to help. I kept peeking out to see people taking their seats. Over four hundred in there, I thought, all the right people. Diti was looking gorgeous as Raina. Guess who designed her dresses for the play? That's right, none other! You know what that means. Once he takes interest in a model on the rise, it is the silver screen sooner or later! In Diti's case it would certainly be sooner. You couldn't say the same about the set and props. It was hideous, to say the least. Whoever did they get for the job! The programme gave his name as Somir Kumar Bhattacharya. There was no mention of the other Bong, Alok. Ah, but there was a buzz in the auditorium. What was all this tamasha of a second production of the same play? In a mix of five Indian languages and Hinglish? And rap? That's the trouble with Bongs and their half baked artistic sensibilities.

Anyway, what mattered in Shaw was the acting. And Diti was going to give it to them. Poor thing, she had a head ache since four in the afternoon, but she was not showing it. Not with her total involvement in the play. You saw that in the dressing room, giving last minute tips to the cast on handling their punch lines. Young people today do not realize that drama must educate the audience. It is not enough to learn your lines, it's how you deliver them. She really has the fire in her belly for this. Shaw in rap indeed! Next you will have hip hop Hamlet! Mrs. Iyer was most supportive. She had arranged sandwiches and pineapple pastries with tea backstage.

Just after the second bell there was a murmur in the auditorium and the sound of people rising. The Chief Guest had arrived. It was the Education Minister. Wrong choice if you ask me. They should have invited the High Commissioner of Great Britain. We could show him how an Indian cast can do justice to Shaw. What could the Education Minister of a state like ours make of *Arms and the Man*? Anyway, there was always the chance that he would go back a bit educated. I would have loved to be seated in the front row to watch his expressionless face through the play. I would read about him at the show in the papers the next day.

In the middle of the last act, when Raina is confronting herself and is ready to admit that she has lived with illusions about her fiancé – some say delusion is the correct word – and the story is ready for the denouement, there was a murmur in the hall and the sound of some people rising again. I peeped through a hole in the front wing to see the Chief Guest leaving, along with his entourage. The Principal and a few senior staff were accompanying the group out. That much for educating the Education Minister! Others in the audience were looking in the direction of the Minister, feet shuffling, irritated at this insensitive behavior. Sergius and Louka paused. Major Petkoff coughed. It was Diti who had the presence of mind to raise her voice over the shuffling feet and continue the scene. The curtain came down twenty minutes later to enthusiastic applause from the front rows. When it went up again to present the cast, Diti invited Mrs. Iyer on stage. She, in turn, invited me to join her. She insisted. The Principal gave us bouquets and distributed token gifts to the actors and backstage crew. He made a pretty speech about drama in education and the continued relevance of Shaw a hundred years later. He asked the audience to go and watch another rendition of Shaw the following week-end. The Principal might have had the last word, but we all knew it was Diti's evening.

The best thing about *Wah Wagah!* was that I was not needed either on stage or back stage. I had done my bit in planting the seed and watering the bud for a while when it sprouted. The gang took over after that. They asked me to design the stage décor and I was happy to do that. I could actually watch the show from the front. And see George Bernard Shaw come to life on stage. I found a place at the back instead, next to a withering fig tree. I could light up there, lean against the tree and take in the whole scene from the seclusion. It felt good. The show was unfolding exactly as it had in my head the first time I read *Arms and the Man.*

I have to thank Diti for that. And Jas for taking me to their rehearsal. I enjoyed working on their scenery. I'd never done any stage stuff before. I hear the audience liked it. The lone newspaper review praised it. It didn't have much to say about the performance. I knew that the Chief Guest walked out before the end. Jas said many others thought of following him, but were signaled back by Princy. They left as soon as the curtain closed. Only the families and friends in front stayed back. And Princy. I felt sorry for Diti. She is a nice girl at heart I think. She doesn't need to prove that to anybody. Jas was right. I couldn't see the play myself. I promised the Wagah gang I'd give them time that evening. They were nearly ready for the opening.

After the second bell there was a murmur and a Mexican wave of heads turning towards the entrance. The English play group was coming in, Diti leading. Jas was with them. She was looking out for me, but I decided to stay put. Mrs Iyer and Diti's mother were there too. They found places kept for them in front by others. Once the show got going I could not see anybody anywhere in the audience. I kept imagining what Diti and her mother and Mrs. Iyer might be whispering among themselves. Half way through I saw the mother leaving, Mrs. Iyer following. Just the two of them. When the show ended they called me on stage. I didn't want to go up, but I was pulled up by four in the gang. The crowd roared a demand for an encore and the gang did the Duty Free Chocolate rap. A final standing ovation and the crowd started to melt away.

The gang started to pack up and put things away. They did a pretty good job with Wagah, I thought. Not bad for a first shot. I sat at the edge of the stage watching the sea of humans turn into a desert of plastic chairs. Two figures remained glued to their seats. Jas was sitting upright, beaming. Diti was teary eyed, sobbing. She was smiling. I went down to meet them. Jas gave me a long tight hug. Diti extended her hand. I took it and patted it with the free hand. She excused herself and left, not without saying we must meet soon for a proper chat. I asked Jas with some nervousness about Diti's mother leaving half way. Did she dislike the show? Oh, nothing like that, Jas said, she just had a headache through the evening.

Drama is just something Diti does on the side. She is a natural and she does not have to prove anything to anybody. There is not much more to do anyway in the confined space of University drama. Been there, done that. She is made for bigger things. It is no surprise that she is not interested in new drama projects after *Arms and the Man*. Drama for who? Ministers of this state? Pearls before swine? The front rows loved the play. That's what matters. Do you know what happened at the opening show of *Arms and the Man* in 1894? I am not surprised you don't. I told Mrs. Iyer the story. While the whole audience was applauding there was a lone oaf out there who chose to boo. When Bernard Shaw was called on stage he addressed the man with great civility and said "Sir, even if I agree with you completely about this play being a dud, we are after all only two against the whole crowd here!"

Diti has a great future ahead of her. She was just waiting to be done with this Shaw thing. I am going to accompany her to Mumbai in the summer. We will camp there and make sure she gets the exposure she deserves. Meanwhile, she is joining a course in animation. Just like her, forever expanding her horizons. It wasn't my suggestion. It was Jas. She was convinced Diti had had enough of drama in college. Been there, done that. Could she join the animation course with Jas and me? Why not, I thought. It's her life. As long as she doesn't...

"As long as she doesn't what?" Jas wanted to know.

"As long as she doesn't get between you and me."

I made up that one real fast. Jas looked me in the eye like nobody else does, like nobody else can. It said take me home.

We walked hand in hand and then arm in arm and then arms around each other. She started to hum a tune. I asked her what it was. She said Diti had taught her the song. It was called Side by Side. She wanted me to learn it, so we could sing it together. Hmmm...a song from Diti. I agreed to go along, but I had to remind her, "As long as she doesn't..."

Jas dug her elbow in my ribs and laughed, "Oh, I'll make sure of that!"

[Over thirty years of working with young people in the theatre through the flagship Summer Project on Theatre (SPOT) has shown that there is a drama queen in every family!]

The Hostage

The gathering in the living room was getting larger steadily. The huddle got tighter. Rohini thoughtfully had the furniture moved against the walls, making more space on the floor. Cotton dhurries were added around the fraying Jaipur carpet in the middle that had been part of the house the last fifty years or more. Appa was seated at the centre of the row against the wall facing the puja room. He had his caste mark on the forehead. An aunt suggested that a lamp be lit in the puja room. There was the slightest rise in the volume of sobs when the oil lamp came to life. The gathering spoke in disciplined whispers, only one at a time, with the right gaps in between. Rohini joined her immediate older brother Hemant at the entrance, receiving friends and relatives, some of them visiting after months and years. An aunt pulled out a framed photograph of Jaggi in his graduating robes and cap, diploma in his hand, beaming. She placed it on the side board and asked for a string of jasmines. Appa nodded and one of the visitors slipped out quietly to look into it.

The small annexe to the living room had a music system and a television set. The door to the room was shut. There were two cousins of Rohini and Hemant inside, keeping track of the news channels continuously, keeping the volume down to the bare minimum.

The thought on everybody's mind was: where was Amma? Nobody actually asked. They respected her need to be by herself, but they wanted to know where she was. An eager neighbour decided to lead the gathering in a bhajan. He began softly, mumbling the first two lines, pausing for the group to pick them up. They did. He completed the stanza. Just then the gathering heard footsteps upstairs. She was coming down to join them. They continued, encouraged by the footsteps. Amma's rubber chappals had a distinctive flip-flup coming down the stairs and a shup-shup going up the stairs.

When Amma entered the living room the leader of the bhajan pressed his palms together, bowed his head and motioned to Amma to take her place next to Appa. Some rose, some moved to make space for her. She held up her hand, suggesting that they stop singing. They did. She turned and walked up the stairs again. The same measured steps, shup-shup-shup-shup. The silence downstairs made her footsteps sound twice as loud. The bhajan was replaced by meditation, punctuated regularly with a sniff or a sob from the women's side.

The door to the annexe opened a few inches at regular intervals and the face of one of the cousins appeared, nodding sideways to say that no progress had been made. They would stay glued to the screen, breaking news every fifteen minutes. The departure of the guests began two minutes later. Amma's command had made it easier for those unsure about the appropriate duration of the visit. They made the needed effort to appear reluctant. They left in ones and twos. A few hung on. It was not clear who among them wanted to stay on and who wanted to display a closeness to the family.

Amma's admonition was not altogether a surprise. All in the family and among close friends knew about her impatience with ritual. Puja, haldi-kumkum, arati, breaking coconuts, bhajans, chants, invocations, all of these she considered infra dig. She did not think much about prayer either. She considered it an expression of human selfishness that people should demand the special attention of the person they called god by an act of prayer. Demanding his attention when in distress she thought was especially distasteful. (Or its attention, as she often stressed, rejecting the gender bias in calling it Him – with a capital H no less.) Demanding the attention in thoughtless ritual prayer was simply infra dig.

⌘ ⌘ ⌘ ⌘ ⌘

When Amma was still Meenakshi in the Ananthakrishna household her parents had wondered about the non-believer streak in her. Where did she get it from? The family elders had blamed the Convent school she was put into by her parents. Ah, but she was unimpressed by the Bible too. The Christian rituals were as foolish to her – and as demeaning – as the Brahmin rituals at home. It is a passing phase, her mother always said, without showing the slightest hint of worry. She found herself saying that for seventeen long years till Meena was out of college. She prayed fervently in secret that it was indeed a phase that would end some day. She was most anxious about finding a husband for her. Meena's regular absence at the annual visit to Tirupati was getting to be talked about outside the household too. What puzzled the family was her disinterest in defending her position in any discussion.

The Ananthakrishna household was famous for the family debates on all things of slightest importance in human affairs – the best way to deal with arrogant auto rickshaw drivers, the inside story behind the hike in milk prices, so soon after the hike in bus fares, the best way to assess real estate offers, the untold behind the scenes drama in the sting operation at the ashram, the correct way to overcome constipation in long journeys, whether to have water before, during or after meals – fifty two debates over fifty two Sunday evening meals when all in the Ananthakrishna household were expected to dine together. Expressions like god-willing, god-only-knows, trust-in-god, god's-grace or god-save-us were usually followed by a glance in the direction of Meena, who responded quietly with a smile. It was a calm and serene smile, with no trace of animosity or hidden meaning. It was called the Meenakshi Magic smile in the family. In fact her mother often said that Meena would win over a prospective groom and his family with her smile instantly, and they would all leave the coffee untouched.

That is exactly how Meenakshi met Nagaraja Rao, and they came to be Amma and Appa years later. She succeeded in persuading Nagaraja's family to keep it simple, and to seriously consider an Arya Samaj ceremony. They thought she was an angel.

When Meena's engagement was announced the family was elated. "I told you she would get around, God bless her!" was the comment of an aunt. Another aunt added, "Marriage ripens the greenest fruits, God bless her!" Later in the evening the Ananthakrishnas visited Meena's grandmother carrying the good news. She acknowledged the glad tidings and added without any prompting that Meena's acceptance of marriage was not to be mistaken as her acceptance of God. It could only be taken as a possible loosening up, with no guarantee of the sort of transformation the parents thought they were seeing.

Ananthakrishna observed cautiously, "As long as there is no embarrassment during the wedding..."

The grandmother was more pragmatic. "After that it is their headache."

Meena's mother was optimistic. "She is a good girl at heart. We all know that. She will be a good wife."

The three of them looked at each other in silence. The grandmother brought the visit to a close with a reminder that it was time for her medication. But she had something to tell the Ananthakrishnas before they left.

"All this godlessness is a fashionable thing. A dangerous fashion. You will not admit it, but Meena is misled. And you are also responsible for that. Prayer and worship are part of good conduct. You modern day parents reason too much. Things should be done first. That's all. Get down there and do it! Reason comes by itself later".

"Maybe that is true. Maybe we were too soft. Maybe..."

"The government should do something about it", grandma continued. "All this freedom of expression is nonsense. It is destroying our culture."

"Anyway, she is getting married now. That is a good thing, no?"

"Look at Anantha here. He was wild as a young man, do you remember?" She then turned her penetrating gaze on the mother. "Who made him human? You! That is what a woman does to the man. That is what a mother does to her children."

Anantha smiled in agreement. The mother bowed her head. The grandmother continued. "It is all right for a son to be godless now and then. God made them that way. But girls? Your own daughter?" She ended with a downward inflexion, head lowered, nodding sideways. The parents did not respond. They understood that the grandmother had not finished.

"When she steps out into the harsh world outside she will know. When she has a tragedy on her hands she will know. She will discover God then." She then slipped an envelope into the mother's hands and excused herself.

The Anathakrishnas bade her goodbye, urging her to come for the engagement ceremony. On the walk back to the car they were both thinking of the same thing. Oh, God! May she never have to be plunged into a tragedy to discover God. When they got home Meenakshi's mother personally phoned all the elders to thank them for their blessings. She prepared a special arati for the array of framed photos in the puja room. She then picked up the gilded frame with the image of the

Lord from the Shri Krishna temple in Udupi and held it close to her heart. It had been given to her by her mother when she set up this home. She would pass it on to Meena for her home.

✂ ✂ ✂ ✂ ✂

Somebody recalled that Jaggi had gone with friends to the One Day International that day because it promised to be an exciting match. It was do or die for the Indian team to save the series. They often walked over to a pub to chill out after a match. Should they call him? An international call? Should they first check with his best friend Somu who had not been selected for the Ozie assignment? He might still be in the office. The telephone rang. It was Somu. He confirmed what the TV channel had reported, that there were four Indians among the thirty and odd customers trapped inside the pub. And then he added...Jaggi was in there. Almost immediately he asked to be excused. He was rushing to the CEO's office to join a team that was acting on the emergency. Among other things they were working on gaining access to the Minister for External Affairs, who was at that time out of the country.

After the initial immobilizing silence of a whole minute the family had burst into action. Phone calls to loved ones, e-mails, google searches, calls to the TV station and motorbike trips by Hemu in all directions. The Puja room was opened. Appa laid himself prostrate.

Rohini went upstairs to give Amma the news, wondering how to wake her up if she had already retired. She was awake. She had taken out a fresh sheet of canvas, pinned it on the board and set it up on the easel. Amma was going to paint through the night. She signaled to Rohini to enter and sit on the stool next to the easel. "Meditation", she explained. Rohini knew she had to obey. She would find the right opener soon enough.

She asked, "What are you going to paint, Amma?"

"I was thinking of something from memory, but now I have another idea."

"From your memory? Like what?"

"Oh, I just remembered a meeting between a mother and a daughter. A meeting and a chat. I thought it might make a nice picture."

"Your mother and you?"

"Maybe. Maybe not. These things don't have to be exactly the way they were. This is not a history textbook. It is a painting." She asked Rohini to wait on the stool and went to the steel almirah that opened only with a grunt from Amma and a krabalanng in response from the almirah. She reappeared with something in her hand that looked like a slim book wrapped in several layers of a finely woven stretch of cloth. There was a thin golden ribbon tied around. She placed the book on Rohini's lap and asked her to open it. "Muslin", she said. When unwrapped it was easily the length and width of a sari. "You don't get muslin of this quality anymore."

Rohini gasped. Inside the wrapping was a gilded frame with the image of the Lord from the Shri Krishna temple in Udupi. This image of Lord Krishna...In Amma's steel almirah? She looked up at Amma, the unspoken questions in her eyes.

"For you", said Amma. "It was given to me by my mother before I got married. It is yours now."

"You kept it in the almirah all the time?"

"The almirah was also given to me by my mother. It will be yours."

"What should I do with this...?" She left the sentence unfinished.

"The god? Or the photo frame with the image of a god? Up to you. It is yours now."

Rohini wanted to wrap up the frame once again with the stretch of muslin, but Amma stopped her. She asked Rohini to keep the photo frame on her lap, facing Amma, and sit erect. That would be her painting. Rohini with god on her lap. Rohini was thrilled, but she remembered that she was up there only to give Amma the news about Jaggi in the Melbourne pub. She had to return downstairs. There were other chores expected of her. She asked Amma if she could return in half an hour. She would spend all the time with Amma then. What brought her upstairs, Amma asked. Rohini went blank. She could not remember a word of what she had rehearsed in her mind. Amma made it easier for her.

"Jaggi is in the pub, is he not?" Before Rohini had caught the words she continued, "Bad news, is it not?". In one burst, exactly like the news reporters on TV downstairs, Rohini gave Amma the entire update – the pub, its location, the number of people trapped, the number of gunmen, the stalemate in negotiations, the warning shots fired, the mobilization of security forces, the helicopters overhead, the diplomatic channels working overtime – she was sobbing profusely by the time she finished. Amma raised her from the stool and drew her to the divan. She held her close. She saw Rohini holding the photo frame close to her heart. When the sobbing stopped and Rohini thought she was ready to go back Amma asked if anything was known about the gunmen. Rohini did not know. Amma asked her to look out for a specific detail. Were they doing this in the name of their race, or in the name of their god. It would make a difference to the way it ended, she said.

She picked up her brushes, stood them in an old enameled army mug she had kept for thirty five years, fixed her gaze on the blank canvas, and spoke to Rohini behind her back. "Come up whenever you can. I will make a start without you."

Rohini dashed off downstairs. The door to the annexe was open. The cousins were in a huddle with the small group that had remained. The gunmen had been identified. They belonged to a fringe group that wanted to cleanse Australia of yellow livered Asians who were multiplying like sewer rats on their soil. The group called themselves White Light, and had become prominent in the past year for their acts of vandalism. They claimed to be part of a global network of Neo-Nazis and had warned the public that their true might would soon be known. There was a video clip that had gone viral and was playing again and again in all the channels. It was taken by one of the gunmen and instantly relayed by their leaders in an unknown location to three television channels. The clip showed two of the masked men with vicious looking hand guns pointing at two hostages on the ground, kneeling, their heads touching the floor. One of the TV news reporters identified the guns as Glock conversion assault carbines, claiming a fistful of brownie points for being the first to find out. The camera zoomed in on one of the gunmen who fired a short burst of three shots and wounded a hostage in the leg. Even as the hostage screamed out in pain the gunman barked a warning at the camera that the next shots would be at the heads of both the men on the floor. They claimed that at that very moment the nation-wide congregation of White Light was rising to rid their sacred soil of the scum if they did not leave on their own accord.

⌘ ⌘ ⌘ ⌘ ⌘

When Meenakshi and Nagaraja returned from their honeymoon there was much curiosity in the Ananthakrishna family about the couple breaking journey in Guruvayur on their way back from the backwaters. Had the Rao family finally succeeded where both Mount Carmel Convent and Tirupati Devasthana had failed? At the lunch hosted by the Ananthakrishnas the conversation was steered by Meena's mother towards Guruvayur via elephants in Thekkady and Thrissur Pooram. "Tell us about your visit to the temple", she finally said. Nagaraja picked up the lead and had lots to say about the spiritual peace one experienced inside the temple. When he paused to ask for some more of the hot rasam, she turned to Meena and asked, "And you?" The Rao family had their eyes on the banana leaf. All eyes of the Ananthakrishna family turned to Meena.

"Oh, I just wanted to find out more about the temple traditions", she replied briefly.

"Among the holiest of the holy shrines of South India."

"And the most orthodox too", was Meena's quick response.

"Steeped in tradition", added Anantha.

"The traditions that made Gandhi go on a fast. I wanted to find out more about that."

The topic of Guruvayur came to an end. The senior Mrs. Rao, Nagaraja's mother, glanced at Mr. Rao, cleared her throat and said she simply had to make an observation. Oh, here it comes, thought Mrs. Ananthakrishna. All eyes were now turned on Mrs. Rao.

"Meenakshi is so well informed. She is sensitive and yet level headed. She is precious." And then Mr. Rao the senior, added a line. "We are so happy that she has come into our home. She lives up to her name as the compassionate one, as the carrier of burdens and hope."

"We got to know her really well through the honeymoon." Mrs. Rao was about to stand to make a statement. Mr. Rao held her back. In their times it was not common for newlyweds to take off on a honeymoon after the wedding. If a couple did choose to do so it was not uncommon for the groom's parents to be invited to accompany them. Mrs. Rao had made a point before the dessert was served. All eyes were now turned on Meenakshi. They saw the Meenakshi Magic.

Meena had something more to say about Guruvayur, but held back. No matter, she had brought traditional Malabar saris and veshtis for both pairs of parents from the temple town. They were displayed when the beeda was brought out. The gifts were greatly appreciated. The hearty welcome-back lunch, too, was much appreciated.

The next day was spent in packing. It was not easy vacating her room in the Ananthakrishna home. What to take, what to leave behind. Her mother kept reminding her that she was always welcome to return for visits whenever she wished to, and that things could be shifted by and by. Meenakshi said she would like to be left alone to concentrate on the essentials. Her mother decided to go down and get some buttermilk ready. In fifteen minutes Meenakshi had put her things together for the shift. She took a photo frame wrapped in muslin from the deep end of her wardrobe and put it on top of the pile in a steel trunk. She was all set for her new role as home maker in a new address. Just as she was about to close the lid of the trunk she heard her mother call from downstairs. "Don't forget the Sri Krishna photo!"

⌘ ⌘ ⌘ ⌘ ⌘

Amma wished to paint Rohini. She had no difficulty in making a start without Rohini on the stool. She had a pencil sketch of Rohini seated in meditation under the hood of a gigantic seven headed serpent. The eyes of the serpent were to be blotches of white to suggest jasmine flowers. This was a mere bottom one third of the canvas. The rest of the frame had a long length of fine cloth, much like Dhaka muslin, twisted, changing direction, changing hue with every twist, partly wrapping the girl and the serpent, and then forming a cloud of snarled cloth over the rest of the frame above the serpent's head. Defying convention of placing the focus of a picture in the upper right hand quadrant of a frame, she had a radiant face in the lower one third of the frame, right in the middle.

There were loud shrieks from downstairs. Amma stopped, her brush an inch from the canvas. She held it there till the shrieking gave way to sounds of urgent mobilization. Hemu and three others could be heard making phone calls. Appa was groaning in a way nobody had heard before. He was seeking the urgent intercession of the ever benevolent Vishnu-Krishna in all of the shrines in four corners of the land. Amma put the brush away in the mug, not before washing and wiping it clean.

Rohini rushed up, breathless. She was distraught. Her voice was choking. The pub had been stormed by a crack anti-terror squad. They had taken the rear service entrance and burst in through the micro brewery door, always kept locked from the inside. In panic the gunmen had killed the two hostages on the floor and three others before being riddled themselves. The Commandant had just appeared before the scores of TV and press journalists and issued a brief statement. It was over. All the gunmen were killed. Five hostages had died. The rest were safe, unhurt. He assured them a more detailed report as quickly as possible, after the urgent mopping up and follow up tasks were done.

"Jaggi is safe", Rohini announced excitedly. "Five dead", Amma replied, her face emotionless. Rohini did not hear her. She continued, "Jaggi was not one of the five. He and his friends dropped to the floor and crept under a table as soon as the first shots were fired. Our prayers were answered."

She stopped, seeing Amma motionless. "Our god...answered our prayers. Five others died." Amma drew Rohini to herself and cupped her face in her palms.

The Invocation

Have you heard of the village of Rampur? You must have. No matter which part of India you come from you will know Rampur. Rampur, Rampura, Ramapuram, it is known by slight differences in the way the name is sounded, but it is Rampur all right, the abode of Lord Ram. My maternal cousin who works in the official labyrinth of the State Information & Broadcasting Department as a Documentation Officer, Grade II, tells me that there are six hundred and forty Rampurs listed all over India. The people in the South of India have the practice of adding the sound 'aah' at the ends of names, so it is called Ramapura. In the same way that I am called Ajaya there. I have given up trying to get them to say Ajay. Oh, yes, I am often asked if I should really be called Sharm then. But returning to the abode of Ram – or shall we say, Rama – six hundred and forty is a good score, right? My cousin is not sure about the exact number. It could be more, but certainly not less. It is not always clear what the exact connection to Lord Ram might be. Was he born there? Did he pass that way on his journey from or back to his kingdom? Is that where he is expected to establish his post-retirement dwelling? There is not a town in my part of India where the Ram-Lakshman-Sita trio did not set foot at one time or another. You will be taken to the spot where the Lord washed his feet, you will watch a sunset sitting on a rock just the way brother Lakshman did, missing home, you will smell the burnt ash at the spot Queen Sita set up her temporary kitchen. Needless to say, there are dozens of ponds where they bathed, the secret to their ever-fresh countenance in every picture frame.

There are variations to the basic, of course. Ramachandrapuram is an example. And Ramnathpur. The one I like is Ramrajyapur. It gets it absolutely right. By thinking of their own wretchedly decayed habitat as the abode of Ram, they are dreaming of it turning into a Ramrajya some time in the not too distant future. They all dream the same dream. The landless farmer as much as the landlord, the goatherd, the pawnbroker, the kirana shop owner, the toddy seller, the ironmonger, the barber and the oil miller, not to forget the temple priest who keeps everybody's dreams alive. The annual Ramlila helps. For those ten days at least the streets look brighter, and the townsfolk do not mind the soaring prices of essentials for the celebration. Not knowing when the Lord's homecoming once for all will be, they make the most of the annual visitation. In the not too distant past Ramlila also served to lift certain barriers of movement across sections of the community. Craftsmen and performing artists of that other faith, whose name we are not supposed to take, were ardent participants. In more recent times there has been some change. People of that other faith are being kept out. Ramrajya has taken on another meaning.

At least one Rampur we must all know has been famous for generations of moviegoers watching Hindi films. The best knives in the country are made there. Ah, yes, the Rampuri. The craftsmen, they say, are all with surnames of that other faith, the ones who don't have a place in Ramrajya. The knives are used in the movies by villains who have surnames we don't mind uttering. There are at least two categories of villains. The fair skinned ones belong to the upper echelons. They are the plotters and schemers who live in mansions with huge dining tables and a grand piano next to a bay window. Then there are the dark skinned ones, who are seen in the narrow streets and alleys. They are the ones who flick the Rampuris open, carrying out the jobs given to them. The dark skinned villains must be oily-faced, and they must have scruffy hair. They prosper on the crumbs thrown by the mansion dwellers. There is a further distinction. The lowest echelons have even larger numbers of the dark skinned. They survive on the crumbs thrown by those carrying the Rampuris. In the name of the Lord.

The movies show us the streets of Bombay quite realistically, especially the people inhabiting them. They get it right. The villages in Bombay movies are what the makers of those movies imagine them to be. In the villages with the name of Rampur we do not have narrow streets and alleys. There are narrow bunds between plots of land and cow paths between hamlets.

⌘ ⌘ ⌘ ⌘ ⌘

It was my second year in the field. In the first year I commuted from the extension centre in town, spending three to four days each time in the cluster of project villages. When I was given charge of a project it seemed better to stay there and come into town once a fortnight or so. It was fine. I was not married and had no ties to the town. Ramnaraindasji had a brick and mortar home at the edge of the hamlet. He offered to put me up in a spare room at the back. Ramnaraindas had the second largest land holding, but was the most influential member of the community. All the locals called him Raman-bhaiyya. Ramnaraindas didn't come easily on the tongue. He insisted that I call him Ramnanarain. I settled for Raman-bhaiyya. He said he had good relations with his friend in the city office, the Programme Manager, and it would be no trouble at all my staying in his house. His friend in the city, the Programme Manager, was a seasoned field officer, and advised me against it. I had to stay with the people we served, not with the people they served, and it would be best to stay as close to their section of the village as possible. There was a narrow gulley between the two sections of the village. The villagers remembered their grandfathers telling them that it used to be a stream long ago, when they were themselves little boys. It was dry the last thirty years or more, with thorny bushes and rocks. The gulley formed a natural line of separation between the two sections. I had to walk up a couple of kilometers to a sandy spot to cross over from one side to the other.

The families on our side of the gulley were landless sharecroppers. There were forty nine families in six hamlets. Three of them had families that had lived there as long as they could remember. They belonged to the same community that was spread over a belt nearly forty miles between two towns along the District road. The families lived on land that was shown in the government records as a registered hamlet. Nobody knew who the land of their hutments belonged to. The other families had migrated there about thirty years ago from the foothills in the north-west. Their forefathers had been given access to the forests, which sustained them in many ways. Some of their livelihood was also from collecting produce from the forest and supplying them to nearby villages and towns. These included wood resins, honey and wax, a variety of leaves and the wild flowers that went into the local brew. One day a party of government officials visited them and gave them six days to move out. The entire area was going to be fenced off for a very important project that would bring prosperity to the whole District. They were given a packet of money and two bags of grains each. The party drove off, not without the reminder. Six days. The families dispersed in three directions. One group decided to try its luck in Rampur.

The two communities in the six hamlets were different, of course. They had their dialects, their own cooking and eating habits, their customs and their songs and dances when there was any occasion to celebrate. They had two things in common. First, they were desperately poor and in perpetual debt. Simple arithmetic showed the truth of the matter and that this was no movie script. The second thing they had in common was something the government records had blanked out, because it did not exist in the State, except in the minds of troublemakers from outside, like the staff in our programme. They were the untouchables. Every person, every family and every form of livelihood in every village in the State had clearly marked stations in the monumental stairway to heaven. Oh, yes, the State records listed them. People could move about the stairway freely during the day, left and right, up and down, carrying out their occupations, as long as they knew where to return at the end of the day. The untouchables had no place in the stairway. Their place was on the other side of the gulley. Ghoos-basti, they called it. If you didn't know, ghoos is the bandicoot rat. The word is also used generally to mean vermin.

⁂ ⁂ ⁂ ⁂ ⁂

They said that Raman-bhaiyya had two faces. Actually he had many more faces. He was a pleasant and agreeable person when he was reclining on the charpoy in front of his house. He was always the first to greet you from the distance. Ram Ram! Could there be any other greeting in these parts? It was another face at the back of his house, where the barn was located, and he was overseeing the farm labour early in the morning and at dusk. The labour was never met at the front of the house. And then there was the Raman-bhaiyya at the temple festival and the Raman-bhaiyya joining the village elders for tea under the old peepal tree.

It was a Monday. I will always remember the evening. I remember it as clearly as the evening I had my first smoke with my school-mates in my home town. It was at the end of the railway platform, behind the goods wagon parked there. This Monday was a first in another way. I had accompanied a group of villagers from across the gulley for a meeting with Raman-bhaiyya. He had called two others from the village council to join the meeting. It would be at his home. It was not a formal Panchayat meeting, he had said. It was just a meeting. Everybody knew what that meant. Raman-bhaiyya was the Panchayat, the Panchayat was Raman-bhaiyya. The council members had arrived early and were being entertained inside. Our villagers got there in time, but waited at a distance to be called. The sun had just set, and the light was low. Raman-bhaiyya emerged from the house with the two others. The villagers heard them from the distance. "Ohho, the ghoos basti people are here..." I had placed myself at the back of the group. It was to be their meeting, led by one of them. I was accompanying them simply to supply technical details and some statistics, if at all needed. Raman-bhaiyya saw me as soon as he sat on the charpoy and signaled to me to come forward. There was no Ram Ram, just a wave of the hand. I gestured to the group, in turn, to move forward, keeping my place behind them.

The meeting. It was finally taking place. But first, I must tell you a little bit about things that happened before the meeting.

Our programme in Natural Resources Management had identified this group of hamlets for a project for more than one reason. It was to be a convergence of multiple efforts – rejuvenation of the land, generation of water resources, alternative income generation and livelihood, skill development, and community development towards self-sufficiency. It was a dream. It took time for programme staff like myself to realize that the villagers we worked with had no such dream. They do not dream and cannot dream. They take part in all our group activities willingly, but go back to a home that does not permit dreaming. We persist. I will admit that there were times when I wondered why I was persisting. It was beginning to feel like playacting. And I could see in their eyes that it was playacting for them too.

Things changed when we had an unexpected visit by four families from the forest community. They decided to reconnect with the branches that had migrated here. Among this community it was not unusual for groups of families to seek out other families for a reunion. They had carried three wild pigs with them, still seen in good numbers in their parts. They had also picked up a supply of roots and spices. I was invited to the reunion. So were the families of the other community in the hamlet. There was singing and dancing till late at night. I had never had wild pig meat before. The body fat is all that is needed to roast it. The spice mix is just rubbed on later. It was a blissful night.

The visitors were up early the next morning, surveying the land all around the hamlet. When they returned they asked to see me. I went down to meet them. I saw that it was a large gathering. Over forty families were present. I was taken directly to the oldest member of the visiting group. I could see from the silver amulet on his right arm and the twin tiger claws below the beads on his neck that he was a revered elder of the tribe. He was playing with a Y-shaped greenstick in his hand. He wanted to know what our programme had set out to do, and how we were going about it. It sounded like an interrogation, and I was not sure I liked it. I responded as respectfully as I could. He listened respectfully too. He then invited me to step outside and follow him. I did, and so did all the others gathered there. We walked about a kilometer due West and stopped at a clump of trees. They were at the edge of a large patch of land covered densely with shrubs. These shrubs produced red seeds that looked like medicinal tablets. Children from the towns loved to collect them and string them as beads. By now I had found out that the leader's name was Jakha. The name rang a bell. In our town office there was a slim volume on the bookshelf on the flora of the region and the links to the local cultural traditions. It was called an ethno-botanical study. I had seen the word for the first time. Jakha was mentioned prominently in the book. There was very little Jakha did not know about trees. He asked us to wait under the trees. He walked into the shrub land about fifty meters, and came out with a palm full of dry leaves. He got us to sit down, and rubbing the leaves between his palms he let a powdery pile flow on the ground. He then went into a meditative trance. All the chatter and murmurs stopped. There was absolute stillness in the group. About two minutes later Jakha arose, and walked with slow, measured steps in the direction of the village. He was holding the greenstick in his two hands with the joint leading him forward. He stopped when he felt a quiver in the greenstick, the joint dipping an inch or two. Jakha dropped the greenstick at that spot. He turned and looked at us, very stern. Then a big toothless grin broke over his face. He pointed to the spot and proclaimed that we had all the water we would ever want.

The digging commenced soon after that morning excursion. Nobody went to work in the fields across the gully. The landlords waited the whole day and were furious. When they did not turn up even the next morning a small patrol was sent across the gully to see what the bandicoots were up to. They were greeted by a group of excited women who were taking food up to the digging site. The timing was perfect. When they reached the site Jakha was just pulling up a rope with a pot full of water from the excavation. There was a loud cheer from all. Jakha raised his hand, asking for silence. He unloosed the pot from the rope and held it between his knees. He scooped out a palmful of water and spread it over his face, blinking his eyes. The second palmful was allowed to drain out between the fingers. He rubbed the last few drops against the four fingers with his thumb. He took out a third palmful and sipped the water slowly, rolling it with his tongue. He looked so much like the tea taster I had seen in a plantation years ago. Jakha picked up the pot in his hands. He whooped and jumped into the air, holding the pot high, saluting the sun in the sky. Our villagers had struck water.

The patrol scurried back across the gully, a bit dazed, a bit frightened too. They did not quite know what to make of the ceremony they had just witnessed. They were only aware of a vague sensation of rumbling in the gut.

Our villagers had struck water. Not only that, Jakha showed us many other things. He showed us how to grow trees just above the shrubland, how to ensure a stronger supply of rainwater, how to create a community pond to store water, and how to recharge the groundwater to ensure a never ending supply. The visitors left two days later, extracting promises of a return visit. Jakha announced magnanimously that he was handing over his project to me. There was more merrymaking the night before their departure. I slipped out early and went to the clump of trees and lay down, watching the stars above. I couldn't see them clearly. I was crying.

⌘ ⌘ ⌘ ⌘ ⌘

The meeting. It was finally taking place. It was now nearly three years since the discovery of ground water above the gully. A lot of water had flown above the gully since then, as one might say.

When the group approached the charpoy the two other elders leaned forward and whispered into Raman-bhaiyya's ear. They were alarmed. Our group had two women. It was bad enough Raman-bhaiyya having the vermin at his home, but having two women in the group was going too far, unthinkable. They were not even covering their faces. I have to tell you this. In all the years that I had known Ramnaraindasji, visiting him in his home, served tea by his wife, I had never ever seen her face. It was always covered. I only knew she wore a large ring on the right side of her nose, because it occasionally peeped through the ghungat. And Ramnaraindasji never told me what her real name was. It had to remain Bhabhiji. That, too, was included in my induction and training. And here they were, two untouchable women from across the gully appearing for a meeting, their faces uncovered!

One of the women was Chhaoli. She was a natural leader. The men admitted that ungrudgingly. She was elected to lead the very first self-help group set up by the community. Very pleasant, but very firm. The group first wanted her to lead the discussion at Raman-bhaiyya's home. They decided later that it should be Bhana. Chhaoli would stand by to step in if needed. Raman-bhaiyya was not unprepared. I had informed him the composition of the group when the meeting was agreed upon. I went up to greet the three hosts, announced that the group had chosen Bhana as their spokesman, and withdrew to the back. Raman-bhaiyya called Bhana forward and asked him to sit close to the charpoy. He called for a woven grass mat to be kept for him.

The group had only two points in their agenda. First, they wished to reduce the number of men and women working on their lands. To start with, the number would be halved. They would phase out fully over the next two to three years. Second, they wished to be compensated better for their labour, with either higher wages or a larger amount of grains. Raman-bhaiyya knew this was coming. He remained cool. The two others were flabbergasted, to say the least, and resorted to the choicest abuses pre-reserved for this group. The critical moment had arrived. It was anticipated, but had appeared sooner than expected. How would Bhana and Chhaoli react? Would they shout back? Stage a walkout? They did the group proud by their deft handling of an explosive situation. They sat still, unaffected.

They waited calmly for the elders to run out of ammunition. With a mere nod Bhana sought Raman-Bhaiyya's view.

Raman-bhaiyya succeeded in restoring order and suggested to the two others that they find out what the group would do for their livelihood, and reason with them. Bhana was prepared for this. The group had rehearsed the scene in the hamlet. Bhana rattled it all out – the horticultural project, the compost project, the sheep rearing project, the connections across the projects, the marketing set up for reaching the district towns, the self-help groups to manage the projects and the finances, and the interconnections across all the projects.

Raman-bhaiyaa saw at once that the group was calling the shots. He had seen for some time that the future was bleak for his farm. One son was about to graduate from a college in the city, and was already talking about starting a business there.

The other son, staying with them, seemed to be going the same way, flatly refusing to take any interest in the land. The two others continued to be contemptuous. And abusive. "We will show you" and "You should know where you belong" were the phrases routinely added either before or after the abuses. Raman-bhaiyya knew that they, too, had seen who was calling the shots, but were compelled to appear invincible. He decided to take charge and suggested that now that everybody had been heard, and all points of view known, they should think about it for a few days and meet once again later. He stretched out a hand restraining the landlords when they started to protest. He closed the meeting by observing that the village could be an example to others all around in settling issues in a civilized manner. The group thanked Raman-bhaiyya and rose to leave. I offered my additional thanks to the two others and we started back. It had turned dark and we were out of sight quickly.

Just as we were taking the bend in the path, one of our group tapped me on the back. We stopped and turned to look. Raman-bhaiyya's house was lit and still visible. Bhabhiji had appeared out of the house with a long broom. She carefully swept Bhana's grass mat away to a pit on the side. She then brought a bucket of water and a mug and washed the spot on which Bhana had sat. Raman-bahiyya watched in silence. We turned and walked back in silence.

⁂ ⁂ ⁂ ⁂ ⁂

Festivals of the village temple were colourful events, as they are in all village festivals. The mela that went with the festival drew people from villages all around. You could say that the mela outside the temple attracted them there more than the deity inside. The people from our side of the gully looked forward to the festivals. They did not have gods and goddesses in their faith. They had spirits to take care of them, many kinds of spirits, and they had small shrines dedicated to the spirits. They could be installed anywhere as dictated by the spirits themselves. They were in the unlikeliest of locations. People from the city missed them on their treks in these parts.

At the village temple festivals our people had learned to wait for their turn for everything – the swings and carousels in the fairground, the sugarcane juice, the sweetmeats, the trinkets and garments in the flea market, the popsicle and the cotton candy. Jaggery balls mixed with tamarind were a great favourite. A makeshift tent cinema showed snippets from movie hits for half an hour at a time. A special enclosure was created for our people, curtained off from the rest of the seating. If they were lucky they got the leftover prasad from the temple priest, kept on tendu leaves outside the entrance. They knew the names of deities of all the temples in that belt, but had never stepped inside to see any of them. They collected a colour print copy of the image from the mela grounds each time.

It was different this year. The temple had agreed to hold a special arati exclusively for our people. It would be at the end of the day, after all others had laid their offerings and made their supplications. The temple had overcome objections and gone ahead with the proposal, backed by the Block Development Officer.

It was finally accepted – as long as it was after all others had been give darshan by the deity, and our people were given a glimpse of the deity from the stone steps outside. The prasad would be dropped into their palms, not kept on the ground.

The temple had been in a state of disrepair for over four years. Funds were not coming in, costs were going up, the electrical wiring in the building was decaying, causing the fuses to blow every now and then, and the drainage was badly clogged. In fact people had complained about a foul smell surrounding the temple. The support from the upper castes had been in words rather than in deed.

When the temple priest placed his woes on the desk of the Block Development Officer, he was asked if he had ever thought about meeting people from the other side of the gulley.

"You mean...?"

"Yes, the hamlets with all those projects there."

"But, sir... they are..."

"Yes?"

"They are people who..."

"The people who...?"

The BDO showed the priest the annual report filed by the Cooperative Society registered from those hamlets. They were the people who had the funds to make a donation to the temple. What did he want? A temple decaying to dust because the people served by the deity do not care? Or a temple with a new life because there are people who might care? He asked the priest to go back and meditate before the deity and try to find out what she herself wanted.

⌘ ⌘ ⌘ ⌘ ⌘

It was going to be festival with a difference. The clump of trees at the edge of the shrubland was going to be consecrated. It was to become a sacred spot, a sanctuary, a symbol of faith in the spirits guarding the communities in those hamlets. It was this spot that had set the communities on the path to rebuilding their lives. Bhana and Chhaoli delivered an invitation to Raman-bhaiyya and the village elders, inviting their families as well. They had to come. It was because of their benevolence, they said, that the community had come to be where they were. The Director of our programme was coming in from the big city just for the occasion. The priest was invited too, although there would be no idol to be installed at the site, and no religious ceremony that he could perform. The installation was to be a large solar power generator. It would give them electricity for the projects during the day and light in the dwellings at night. The ceremony at the clump of trees would invoke the spirits of the forest, seeking mercy for forsaking them, inviting them to return and reside in the grove and continue to protect them. The event was a month away, but everybody felt that the invitations had to be sent early. Before they departed Raman-bhaiyya enquired if he and a few others could come over and see the projects first hand before the ceremonial event. Of course, they were most welcome.

A small delegation was constituted to visit the project site. Our people decided that it would be most appropriate if I accompanied the group led by Raman-bhaiyya. It was a party of four. In addition to Raman-bhaiyya and the priest there were two others from the village council. One of them was Balramdasji, known as Balaa-bhaiyya by all. He was generally not seen in village meetings. He held himself aloof because in the village hierarchy he belonged to a community of a higher station than the rest. If he did attend meetings he would sit apart, interrupt often, listen very little and give uncalled for opinions. He agreed to join the party mainly because of his business interests. The projects on the other side of the gully seemed to offer an opportunity.

The first stop would be the home of Chhaoli. The entrance had pictures and charts and paintings on the mud walls that showed it was also where one of the self-help groups met. Bhana seated the group on the floor in front of Chhaoli's home. He excused himself and said he would serve tea. Chhaoli took charge and explained how all the projects worked, and how they were held together by the Cooperative Society. I watched her in admiration from my place at the back. Balaa-bhaiyya sat a few feet away as expected, and asked questions as if he knew the answers already. He did not, of course. Chhaoli handled the Q&A very well indeed.

Tea was served. It was time to walk over to the solar project site and, from there, to the sacred grove where the invocation would be held. The guests shuffled and started to move away, led by Bhana. Chhaoli smiled and gestured that I should go up and join the group. She had other things to do. I walked fast to catch up with the rest of them. The group turned back as I approached them. They stood still, looking beyond me. They saw Chhaoli with a bucket of water and a mug. She was washing the spot on which Balaa-bhaiyya had sat.

[The field of Indigenous Knowledge Systems is established and respected today. It developed in parallel with an activist movement to assert the rights of tribal communities to their forest habitat as guaranteed by law, but usurped by powerful forces that displaced them.]

The Lunch

The Cauvery Waters dispute was not getting anywhere. A resolution appeared dimmer year by year. The outgoing Cabinet in Delhi was secretly glad that the monkey was now on the back of a new Prime Minister. The Rajya Sabha arithmetic was coming up. It was opening up a bargaining front with – tadaa! – the Chief Minister of Tamilnadu. She lost no time in calling the Prime Minister. After the perfunctory lines of congratulations she slipped in the issue of the Cauvery Waters among the bargaining chips with New Delhi. The new Prime Minister could only reply that he would "definitely look into it". Everybody understood what that meant. It was not a rejection of the proposition, but it was not an acceptance either.

After the phone call the PM did look into it. He was puzzled. What was the problem? If the Narmada Waters issue could be made a non-issue with a will that found a way, why not Cauvery? The real issue for the PM – and the PMO – was how to make Karnataka and Tamilnadu play with a new set of rules of the game. He decided to invite both Chief Ministers for meetings on the same day, but separated by an hour.

The Chief Minister of Karnataka's appointment was at 10 am. When he arrived at the meeting at 10.04 he found the Prime Minister already seated on one side of the round teapoy. Next to him was standing a gentleman he did not recognize. There was an empty chair on the other side of the teapoy. The Chief Minister entered the room with a Namaste. He was accompanied by a Special Secretary. The PM responded to the CM by looking at his watch. He then signaled to the CM to take his seat. The Special Secretary chose to stand beside the CM. The tea service arrived the moment the CM's body made contact with the chair. The PM opened the conversation. He spoke in Hindi. He extended a warm welcome to the Honorable CM and went on to ask if the rains had arrived in Karnataka. The person standing next to the PM translated it into English. The CM, in his response spoke about the rains not only playing truant, but getting steadily less year by year. The consequences were well known. The crops were drying up, people were not bathing any more, the ponds had turned into football fields, and the CM's car was washed only once a week. The CM's reply was in Kannada.

The PM and his Translator looked at each other. Receiving a nod from the PM the Translator asked if the CM might repeat his response in Hindi. It was the turn of the CM and his Special Secretary to look at each other. A nod from the CM, and the Special Secretary took out a bundle of fresh 500-rupee notes from a bag and handed them over to the Translator. There were protestations from the PM and Translator. The PM managed a "Magar, magar...", promptly followed by "But, but..." from the Translator. By then the Special Secretary had spread out one of the notes on the teapoy, face down. He looked at the CM, suggesting he continue. The CM did continue, in Kannada again, requesting the PM and the Translator to look into the currency note closely. The Special Secretary took out a large magnifying glass from his coat pocket and placed it over the left side of the currency note where the value of the note was printed.

Speaking for the first time the Special Secretary explained in English that listed on the note were fifteen official Indian languages other than Hindi, alphabetically arranged. Indian scripts arranged alphabetically? Ah, by phonetic English, of course.

"Achcha..." mumbled the PM, followed promptly by "Good..." from the Translator. The Special Secretary then produced a translation of the CM's response about rainfall in Karnataka, which was rendered into Hindi immediately by the Translator. The PM nodded. The CM nodded back. The Translator and the Special Secretary smiled at each other. They were both from the Indian Administrative Service and translation to and from English came easily to them.

"Achcha achcha..." mumbled the PM again, this time with a grin, followed quickly by "Good good..." from the Translator, also with a grin. "Would the Honorable Chief Minister like to take a bath in the annexe?" Hindi-English-Kannada, and the CM replied that since he was returning the same afternoon via Chennai, he would take a shower in Chennai. They had all the water anyway. Kannada-English-Hindi.

At this point, the Principal Assistant to the Principal Secretary walked into the room, duly half bent, carrying a folded A-5 sheet of paper on a silver tray. He left as soon as the PM picked up the paper. It was an urgent message from the Chief Minister of Tamilnadu which reminded the PM that not a bucket of Tamil water can be made available to any Kannadiga for any use, and that the Honorable PM must not make any offer to Karnataka on behalf of Tamilnadu without prior consultation and consent. Hindi-English-Kannada again and the Chief Minister of Karnataka was advised to take a shower in Delhi rather than in Chennai.

The PM then suggested that a solution to the Cauvery dispute may be found once and for all if the two Chief Ministers met directly. The CM hesitated with "Aadre...". It was followed promptly with "However..." from the SS and "Parantu" by the Translator. "Achcha!" said the PM triumphantly and rang a silver bell kept on the teapoy. "Sirf paanch minit", he assured the CM. The SS whispered into the CM's ear that the geyser was being switched on and that the shower room would be ready in five minutes.

The next three minutes were spent in small talk. While the CM went on about the expansion of the international airport in Bengaluru, the PM was stressing the importance of cleaning up the Ganga. They stuck to Kannada and Hindi. The SS and the Translator decided to let their two masters be. Kannada-Hindi jugalbandi.

"We have named it after the ruler Kempegowda."

"Names are very important. Varanasi is any day better than Benaras."

"Or KIAL."

"Or Kashi."

"It is ready to take a 380."

"Actually it should not take more than 6 months."

"But your civil aviation authorities in Delhi are taking their own time over it."

"These Dilli-wallahs are like that. They say a minimum of three years.

"We have to do something about that."

"I will have to do something about it myself."

"How can clearing a file take such a long time?"

"We have cleared slums in six hours and put up shopping complexes there."

"You can do it?"

"The fruits of hard labour are always sweet."

"The mango season this year was bad."

"The litchis from Muzzafarnagar were late this year."

"They say it is because of..."

"You know the reason. Irresponsible government. But we will deal with that soon."

"That will be so nice."

"Achcha... You will have lunch here, I hope."

"Mangoes?"

The CM's eyes lit up. He oozed confidence that the meeting was going well. Just then a gong was heard outside and the door opened to let in the Chief Minister of Tamilnadu. The CM gasped. His eyes got buried between the brows and the cheekbones. He hurriedly placed himself behind the PM. Following the CM of Tamilnadu, called Big Ben in the inner circle, or simply BB, was a retinue that included two men carrying a third chair and two men in safari suits who walked backwards in front of Big Ben. They left as soon as BB was seated. Behind BB, walking in step, was the Secretary General, a post created only in Tamilnadu by BB. Bringing up the rear was a squad of sixteen photographers from the press and eleven TV cameramen.

Pleasantries done, the PM requested Big Ben to be seated. Noticing that the CM was not at his chair he coughed. The CM emerged from behind and stepped up to his chair. All three were seated. The room was ablaze with sunlamps and popping flashes for half a minute. All three on the seats offered smiles that the cameramen wanted. The double door was shut as soon as they left. The three continued to smile.

"Achcha" the PM began. "Ab hum baat kar sakte hain." He was cut short by the Secretary General, who took out a bundle of fresh 1000-rupee notes from a bag and handed them over to the Translator. The PM looked heavenwards and managed a "Phir se, phir se...", promptly followed by "Again, again..." from the Translator. The Secretary General spread out one of the notes on the teapoy, face down. He looked at BB, suggesting she continue. The CM and SS took out one 500-rupee note each and waved them like fans before their faces.

"Jante hain, jante hain" said the PM. The Translator translated, and the currency notes were put back in the bag, not without some unwillingness.

"Achcha" the PM began again. He explained to the Translator that it was now going to be English-Tamil-Kannada. The CM whispered into the SS's ears who, in turn, whispered to the Translator. All right, the Translator agreed that the Kannada translation may come before the Tamil. A whispered protest from Big Ben's SG was relayed via the Translator to the SS, who whispered back that Kannada was alphabetically ahead of Tamil. Two more rounds of whispered protests and it was agreed that it would be Kannada first once and Tamil first once, taking turns. Ah, but they had to start with Kannada.

The PM opened the proceedings, extolling the virtues of a win-win, growth oriented development model by which the States would benefit if the region was strengthened, and the region would benefit if the nation was strengthened. Water would play a vital role in such a grand plan. The states should be given the chance to arrive at a strategy by themselves first. If they failed, the Centre would be compelled to impose a strategy on them. As a matter of fact, it was time to introduce a performance-based reward system in allocations to states. And water... He took a dramatic pause... would be central to any regional development plan. He hoped BB and CM followed.

Hindi-English-Kannada-Tamil.

"Plain water would be fine", said BB, nodding decorously.

"No ice", said CM, nodding a lateral figure-of-eight that meant approval in his part of the country. The Translator nodded to the PM to continue.

"Achcha", the PM replied, and continued. "If the water problem is not addressed, the food security system can only worsen. It is already dangerously fragile. Why so? You can thank the incompetence of the previous government for that. Do we want it to get worse in states that do not subscribe to the government in Dilli? Hmmm? Another meaningful pause. Think about it. Everyday dal-roti may become a luxury. In contrast, look at the sumptuous and nutritious food in every Gujarati home."

Even as the Translator began, BB and CM, along with SS and SG chorused their approval of the PM's message.

"Yes, yes, dal-roti would be fine."

"Yes, a Gujarati thali would be wonderful."

"Is there aam-ras?"

"Shrikhand?"

"And those super thin phulkas?"

"If it is not too much trouble, can we have the khandvi bed-rolls?"

BB and CM rose together to adjourn to the dining room, with elaborate pehle-aap gestures between them. BB relented and led the way, followed by all others, including the Translator. The PM was left behind, seated still. "Is baar kya?" he mumbled to himself and buried his head in his palms.

The Middle

Anna turned sixty five on the twenty-sixth of December. He is called by other names in other branches of the family tree. Appaji, Baba, Appu, Dad and even Pop. In our home he has always been Anna.

Anna was born on the twenty-sixth of December sixty five years ago. His parents thought the baby might arrive on Christmas day. The early waves of labour had actually begun after dinner time, but his arrival was only the next morning, the day some people remember as Boxing Day. It was at the crack of dawn that he announced his arrival sixty five years ago with a yawn. That was him. From the moment of his arrival his was the personality of utmost unexcited detachment. A smart smack on the bottom by the midwife and the yawn turned into a wail. It was only for the required period of half a minute to get all cylinders firing. Once he had demonstrated the engine capacity, the wail settled down to a healthy purring found acceptable by all, and then into the yawn once again. Celebration! The sun came out of hiding five minutes ahead of schedule and lit up the eastern sky outside the labour room. Trunk calls were made and telegrams sent by the designated male members of the household to the predetermined recipients.

Thata, infant Anna's father and, hence, Thati's significant other half, was holding the fort on the home front. He poured himself a tumbler of fresh coffee. As he sat down to take the first sips he realized that he was now jobless. There was nothing more to do. His ten-month project appointment had ended. The women would take over now. Suddenly feeling an emptiness in the midst of joy and celebration all around he put pen to paper to write a middle for The Times on exactly what had flashed in his mind a moment ago. Joblessness at the end of the ten month project. The Times published the middle readily, correcting only a single grammatical error, which Thata did not object to in the least. It was titled *The Rebirth*.

The newspaper printed the middle even before Thati returned home. She remained in her own mother's home for the mandatory four weeks of rest and massage and grandmother's dietary regime. When Thata visited her the evening of the delivery he did not say anything about the middle he had sent off to The Times. As he gazed into the crib for the first sight of his newborn son, he was thinking really about the middle. Baby Anna yawned. Thati finally returned home a week later than four weeks. She was accompanied by the retinue from her home, helping her unpack and settle in. When she finally found time to settle into her favourite diwan, rocking the baby with a newly acquired expertise, she saw an addition to the framed pictures on the wall in front. It was the middle from The Times. Thata explained shyly what it was. She cooed to baby Anna and asked him to look look look. That yawn again.

Thata departed, god bless his soul, when Anna was thirty five. By then he had written ninety nine middles. Most of them in The Times with his by-line, some in two other newspapers, upon their request, but with two pen names created specially for them. He did not make it to a hundred. Thata was methodical to a capital M. He had two sets of his ninety nine middles in two ring binder files. One had them in chronological order, beginning with *The Rebirth*. The other had them by title in alphabetical order. The last pages of both files had an index listing the articles in that file, along with the date of publication and name of newspaper. Ninety nine articles each in the two files.

Thata had prepared for his departure six months in advance. A meticulously crafted will was in place. It was read in his presence to all in the peepal-sized family tree. It mentioned the investments duly transferred to the listed kin, not forgetting two daughters, which raised some eyebrows in some branches of the peepal tree. All taxes had been paid, all loans cleared and all debts recovered. A gratuity was provided for the two servants who had been in the household for over thirty years each. Every movable and immovable asset that could be called his was accounted for. The old Plymouth was donated to the faithful driver to do what he liked with it. He did. A week after Thata's departure he sold it by weight and got himself a second hand Yezdi-Jawa in very good condition with a side car thrown in. The new Hindustan Landmaster went to Anna. Hot masala vadais were served with payasam at the end. Someone asked if what was unfolding might be Thata's hundredth middle. He grinned and suggested that it was time to disperse. They knew that the pain had commenced. He insisted on being left alone when it came. He had reluctantly agreed to the shots, but had ruled out any hospitalization. As the family filed out of the room, still chatting, fighting off the impending gloom, Thata motioned to Anna to stay back. When they were alone, he held Anna's hand and asked him to take out the two files of middles from the almirah. When they were brought to his bed he placed them on Anna's lap and said they were his. Right there Anna decided what he was going to do that night. He would write the hundredth middle for Thata. The Times simply had to print it before he went away. It was not to be. Thata departed before there was even an acknowledgement from The Times.

⁂

Ah, but this is a story about Anna. It was difficult not to remember Thata, god bless his soul. Anna turned sixty five on the twenty-sixth of December. As on any other morning he was in the kitchen at a quarter past five, long before the rest of the family had stirred. He set the coffee filter and cleared the sink, wiping the dishes and returning them to the rack. He had learned very early in married life that the secret of Amma's good mood through the day was for her to catch the sight of a clean sink when she entered the kitchen in the morning. That with the aroma of fresh coffee. The next half hour was spent on meditation with the cassette player softly playing the sound of surf on a peaceful ocean shore. He then sat at his desk to write. There were three things to write in the morning. The first was the entry in his dairy. This was any reflection on happenings the previous day. He had discovered long ago that sleeping over things and writing the next morning brought in fresh insights to the reflection. After the dairy it was the account book. The bills and little slips of paper clipped together through the day now received systematic entries in the leather-bound ledger that held the family accounts since the day their first child started school. The third bit of writing was not mandatory. It was optional and occasional. It was to compose a middle for the newspaper. Anna hadn't written one in over three months. This morning, in a lighter mood, remembering it was his birthday, he thought he would flip through some of his past writing. He took out the two files he had maintained himself, a discipline he had acquired from Thata, and sat down to peep into the collection with the chronological listing. There were sixty five articles filed. He smiled to himself. That was one for every year of his life. The very first one was what he had written on behalf of Thata. Not one of the sixty five had been published.

Anna enjoyed flipping through the file, each article glimpsed bringing back a memory, an anecdote here, an incident there. He put the files back in the book case and sat at his desk again, wondering what to do in the next twelve minutes when it would be time to step out for the morning walk. He took out a pad and scribbled a message for his family in verse and left it on the dining table.

How can one ever miss
A fine morning like this?
A longer walk
No small talk
No park bench analysis

First come first served
Have you not heard?
Steaming idlis
Give me weak knees
Returning early absurd

And then he added a line: *Will be at Manju's and be back by 9. Packet for Pittu in sideboard drawer.*

Actually Anna did not like fuss and ceremony around his birthday – people streaming into the kitchen-dining from all corners of the old bungalow bellowing birthday greetings, manhandling him with hugs and kisses, thrusting gifts into his hands. Of course they meant well, but he felt an unease he could not explain. He had to go along with the cheer and chatter even as he put up with being violated.

The exception was little Pittu. It was an open secret that Pittu was Anna's favourite grandchild. Not having a son himself, and his three daughters presenting him five children between them, all high decibel models, turbo-charged further in their new generation play schools, Anna found a sprout in the garden after his own heart in Pittu. That is the way the family saw it. A grandson-sized son. The family knew that Anna dreaded birthday mornings in the dining room because of the boisterous assertion of belongingness rights. They also saw that Anna was drawn to Pittu because he was different. He was quiet, the antithesis for a child in a house with this street address. He would stand at the back, waiting patiently to catch Anna's eye, and then produce the affected frown that Anna had actually been waiting for from the time he got out of bed. Head slightly bent, the knitted brow, puffed cheeks and pouted lips. It was the invitation. And then Anna would leave the herd and advance on Pittu, crouched, like an old lion approaching a lamb lost in the forest. This lamb was inviting the attack, still frowning, but in delighted anticipation. A mighty roar and Anna would pounce on Pittu, lift him up high and seat him on top of the book case.

The aunts and all the cousins loved Pittu. There was no resentment about the extra ration of attention that Pittu received from Anna. They saw that it was merely attention, not special favours. In the new age joint family that they were there was all round fair play all the time. The family had accepted that Pittu was, well, different. He hardly spoke. In fact he did not speak till he was almost two. It was as if he had waited to grow a full vocabulary in his head, soaking in all the conversation among all in the family, before going public. Visitors to the house saw a quiet little boy who was "seen and not heard" the whole evening. Well behaved, they thought. And then, at a time Pittu thought appropriate, he would open up with something like "The wash basin is down the corridor, on the right". Or "May I switch on the fan for you?"

It did not mean he would continue to chatter after that. He knew when to speak and when to stop. Yes, he was well behaved. He preferred reading to talking. Nobody knew how much he knew. Except Anna. Pittu hardly spoke. Except with Anna.

Sometimes, usually after dinner, when the dining room was quiet once again, Anna would switch on the cassette player and take out his scribbling pad to put down ideas that had lit up his mind through the day. He liked to sit on a thin floor cushion for this exercise. It was not unusual to find Pittu sitting in front of him with his art book. He had taken to the art book when he was five. It was the best birthday present he could ever have received. By the time he was six he had graduated from crayons through sketch pens to water colours. The A-4 size art paper was now A-2. He had a board with clips that could face him at an angle as he sat on the floor to sketch or paint. The sketching in the evening with grandpa would be followed by colouring in his room the next day. Just as the points Anna jotted down would turn into a fleshed out middle the next morning.

It was only when Pittu was seven that Anna noticed something special about Pittu's art. It was quite accidental. Anna had taken some time to start scribbling notes after the music began. Pittu remained still too. When Anna began to write he did what was an old habit of many years. He would mumble words and phrases intermittently as he wrote. That evening it went something like:

Onions...Crotchety old woman... No change saar...Cow dung on pavement

As he wrote he saw that Pittu seemed to be punctuating his strokes on the sheet with pauses in somewhat the same way he was mumbling and writing. When it was time to close he asked Pittu if he would show him what he had sketched. Pittu pushed it forward readily. He had sketched what appeared to be a street scene with a huge cow occupying most of the sheet. Under its legs you saw a woman on the pavement, seated on a mound of vegetables that looked like...onions. She had three inch long canines, and she was displaying them like a snarling dog warning intruders about its territory. Anna gazed at the sketch for a full minute, unable to take his eyes off it. When he looked up he saw Pittu, head bent, the frown, the pouted lips. There was a moment of understanding between them that had to remain unspoken, undefined. Finding words for it would be futile, even ruinous. It had to remain between grandpa and grandson. They never talked about it ever.

One day, not too long after, Anna was out in the verandah by three in the afternoon. He looked down the road every minute for the sight of Pittu's school bus. When it turned the corner at the bakery Anna went up to the gate to receive Pittu, helping him with his bag. Hand in hand they entered the verandah where Pittu took off his shoes before entering the house. Anna said he would wait there for Pittu to change, have his afternoon buttermilk and snack, and then join him for a chat.

The chat was going to be about Pittu's studies. The class teacher had sent a message to his mother about his unsatisfactory marks in Science and Maths. The school was surprised at this, because Pittu's cousins were toppers in these subjects.

There was a particular problem with Pittu's progress in Science and Maths. He was not submitting his home work, which could only mean he was not doing his home work. Anna sat on the swing in the verandah and thought about a tactful opening of the topic. He decided not to talk about the complaint from his class teacher at all. He would play some science games and then find an entry point to talk about his studies.

Anna did find the entry point soon enough. He struck a neat connection between a favourite game of his and the science taught in school. His own science teacher in school had taught him this game. It was called "How can you have a straight line in a round world?" Through the game Anna found that Pittu really enjoyed his science classes. The Maths too. And the home work? Pittu did the home work too. But he did not turn them in. On probing Anna learned that Pittu did not turn in his home work because he liked to do the home work his way, and not the way the whole class was expected to do it. Would he show the home work to Anna? Of course! He would love to show them to Anna! And off he went upstairs to bring a year's home work down.

Anna was stunned speechless. All his Science home work was in pictures. Pencil sketches, charcoal sketches, crayons and sketch pens, even a few in water colours. There was one of a gigantic candle. At the centre of the flame was a tiny human figure, which was himself, unscathed, while mosquitos trying to strike him like fighter jets were burnt dead at the outer layer of the flame. There was one with an omelette sizzling on a black slab of stone in the sun while a fluffy pup was curled up comfortably on a white slab. Pittu explained with ease the difference between heat as a property and temperature as a quantity. And the solar eclipse had Pittu and his cousins playing hide and seek. That mischievous frown. And that moment of unspoken understanding once again. Curious, Anna asked if Pittu had any other pictures. Any favourite ones? He did, indeed. Would he share them with Anna? Another dash upstairs and there they were. Pictures for Anna's middles, constructed from his after dinner mumblings. Anna was amused. But in a strange way he felt within himself that he was also honoured. This bouquet from Pittu was most precious.

⌘ ⌘ ⌘ ⌘ ⌘

Ah, but this is a story about Anna. He turned sixty five on the twenty-sixth of December. The family had got used to his absence on the morning of his birthday. Amma was the only one who greeted him in their bedroom before he set the coffee and left the house. Any celebration would only be in the evening. This birthday was no different. When he returned from Manju's after a sumptuous idli breakfast the house was quiet again. Just as he had expected, just as he had wished. The children had left for school. The girls had left for work, the menfolk dropping them on their way. Amma had left for the temple and vegetable market. There was a vase of fresh flowers on the dining table. Around it were hand crafted greeting cards from all, and a larger card saying "See you in the evening!" Anna was in no hurry to examine the cards. He peeped into the sideboard drawer to see if Pittu had taken his gift. He had. And he had left a return gift for Anna, a hurried pencil sketch on a sheet from a writing pad. It was a sketch of the back of a large envelope, the flap opened. Peeping out of the envelope was a man's face and neck and a waving hand. The man was balding and grey on the sides. He wore glasses and had a wide smile. The envelope itself...it was large. Stood up against a two storeyed bungalow it covered half the verandah and most of the ground floor bay window. Anna smiled to himself. He poured himself a coffee, picked up the newspaper and sat at the head of the table for a leisurely read. It was then that he noticed an envelope among the greeting cards. It was a morning courier delivery. A few more sips of coffee, and Anna reached out for the envelope. It was from The Times. Anna put it aside. He decided to open it only after he had read the newspaper and had his bath. He sipped his coffee with a new determined leisure.

The Necktie

The impatient honking outside the gate did not bother Meera. She held Panchu back and insisted on giving him one last head to toe. She reminded him of his own tales from the NCC days and the rigorous inspection by the CO before ceremonial parades. He liked that. In a resolute show of going along he snapped to attention on her command, allowing her to go all around, straightening a crease here, flicking off the lint there, and finally centering the knot of the necktie. Thirty five years being married to the man, and Meera knew that behind the good humoured gesture of obedience Panchu was straining at the leash to rush out and join the gang.

There was that honking again. "Stay!" Meera commanded, without raising her voice, and went to the window to announce to the noisy bunch that Panchu would be with them in exactly two minutes. Then she rushed off to the bedroom. Half enjoying the game, taking the place of the Labrador, Panchu stayed, but "at ease" by now. He heard the clang of the Godrej door opening, and before he could bark "Move to the right in single file" she had reappeared. She had another necktie in a cellophane wrap in her hand. And a big smile on her face. "Here, wear this at the reception", she said. "I know how much it means to you... See if she remembers it!"

Aah, that necktie! The yellow polka dots on the blue silk, the twill weave, the Italian label at the back...Panchu was immobilized for a few moments. Then he heard Meera whispering, "Handsome brute!" A tight hug, nuzzling her neck, and he was off. Meera stood at the doorway and watched him prancing to the waiting Innova.

He looked so much like their son Boney when he was still in school, running off on Saturday mornings to the cricket club without breakfast. She saw Bajji, Gullu and Viks waving at her from the car. She waved back, and then decided to walk up to the car to give the boys an important message. "Make sure he shaves the hair off his ears before the reception!" A big hurrah from inside the Innova and it zoomed off on its three hundred kilometer journey.

If Meera were to be invited to write an essay on what made a robust marriage she would definitely include a paragraph about the discovery of G-O-D in their lives. And how that is so crucial for true happiness in married life, a joy far deeper than anything anybody can get from album events like the first vacation together, that trip to Brindavan Gardens or Kodaikanal or Darjeeling or Agra, with the photo taken in front of Taj Mahal. It would be on the importance of nostalgia in a couple's life. Talking about the Good Old Days at least once a month is like a vital dietary need. (Isn't that where the word vitamin comes from?) It can be resorted to as frequently as needed. Panchu and Meera had reserved the second Saturday of each month for just that. No other social engagement could take its place. Standard practice called for a movie, followed by dinner, followed by hot chocolate fudge in their favourite ice cream parlour, topped with lots of rich nostalgia playing GOD.

Their circle of friends, even relatives, knew that it was pointless inviting them for anything on the second Saturday. That made a total of nearly four hundred of those special Saturdays since they launched the regimen. They had saved up for a trip to Niagara Falls for the four hundredth. They missed the date only twice – once when Meera was stranded in Pune with a missed flight, and once when Panchu had to have his hernia repaired. On that second occasion the couple had the session in the hospital room on the following day, a Sunday.

Meera could not count the number of times Panchu had regaled her with the story of the gang's trick riding in front of the girls hostel. On motorbikes, of course, not bicycles. Or the night spent at the police station playing rummy with the night shift cops. How they landed there was a story in itself. Or the six-hour walk in the rain to escort two girls home because of the bus strike. Or the herding of twenty water buffalos into the Principal's bungalow. Or the parade of donkeys in the student protest against a corrupt minister. Meera had her treasure chest of stories too. The all time favourite was the one of seeing Panchu for the first time standing obediently at the corner in the Principal's room. She asked him to fetch a glass of water. Realizing that the girl had mistaken him for the Principal's orderly, Panchu opened the fridge in the room, gave her a bottle of lemonade, and went back to his place. The Principal entered just when she was taking the last gulps...and Panchu had slipped out of the room.

⁂ ⁂ ⁂ ⁂ ⁂

At the half way mark the Innova stopped at a dhaba for a paratha lunch and chai. Naturally they remembered Nair's Den outside the campus. Most evenings would end with a stroll to Nair's for the regulation masala bun and chai. Nair also served the best mutton biriyani a student's pocket money could buy. People came to Nair's from miles around for his biriyani. The first week of every month had the Den overflowing with hostel students. The numbers increased year by year as Nair's reputation spread to other campuses. People never stopped wondering how he managed the supply. Not once did he send any group back without feeding them. From about six in the evening till a little after eleven it was one long biriyani-fest. After a week or so, with the pocket money down to less than half, it was back to masala bun and chai. After eleven the clientele at Nair's was somewhat different.

The narrow lane behind Nair's led to the Railway Colony. The area in between was called Pulikad. It was the jungle where you might encounter a tigress or two. They stayed mostly in tenements off the lane, but you could occasionally catch a glimpse of the feline form silhouetted against a window frame. Their keepers were usually found slouched against a wall at the start of the street.

The phrase Time Stood Still must have originated at Nair's Den. Not only had the den not changed over thirty and odd years, Nair himself seemed just the same every time the gang saw him. That was about once in ten years. The same sideburns, the same bushy eyebrows, the same grin with the glint from the gold upper pre-molar. The same rough pine wood tables and benches too. The one addition to the den about fifteen years ago was an Inner Chamber with four tiny cubicles, and curtains made from printed bed sheets drawn across the entrances. It was around that time that the college intake of girl students had gone up by fifty percent.

Nair remembered the names of students forever. It must have been because of the ledger he maintained for all the service on credit. Cash down payments were twenty percent cheaper than credits, but at the end of the month the credit payments were easily four times more than cash downs. The last time the gang dropped by, which was about twenty five years after leaving college, Nair had greeted them by their nick names and asked if it would be the usual. That was rum and coke served from an aluminium tea kettle, two plates of masala egg curry and a pile of Malabar Barottas. Nair always enquired about others from the same batch or the same gang of friends. He could be expected to throw in an extra plate of egg curry on the house. Before the gang left he had said "You were the best!" It felt good hearing that from old Nair, putting aside the sneaky suspicion that he might be saying that to all old students. Maybe he liked this gang because they always paid up within the third day of each month.

It was thirty eight years since leaving college! As the gang drove up to the campus they decided that a masala bun and chai at the den was in order before entering the gates. It was a mandatory pit stop. And what a welcome it was from Nair himself! The den was overflowing with alumni, all there with the same idea of a ritual chai before the reunion events got going on campus. But Nair had time for the gang as if they were the only ones he was expecting. He was particularly happy that Viks had joined the trip. He pulled out the ledger to show Viks that he still owed him twenty rupees. He winked as he calculated what the compound interest on that would be.

The highway was surprisingly good, not the two narrow lanes they had in those days, with no shoulders to the tarred surface. If you went off the road for more than thirty yards you qualified as a stunt driver. There were three lanes on either side now, with a divider dotted with flower beds. It was a luxury undreamt when the trip was done in an Austin A-40. The Alumni Association office had very thoughtfully made reservations for as many as possible in faculty homes on campus, and in hotels nearby for others. The gang chose a hotel. The drive was still tiring. Six hours on the road made you want a cold shower, a long drink and an early dinner.

⌘ ⌘ ⌘ ⌘ ⌘

The morning of the Big Day was spent in visits to alumni families who lived in the city. Gifts were exchanged and yarns woven. Lunch was with a large gathering on the verandah of a hotel that offered the best deal for such occasions. The main attraction was that they allowed the hosts to bring their own beer and wine. There would be no drinks on campus at the evening reception. The leisurely lunch followed by a long siesta was just the right preparation for the evening.

The first sight that greeted all visitors on arrival at the reception was the giant shamiana that occupied all of the football ground. It had a semi-circular section at the centre for the speeches and entertainment. Around this were four separate meeting spaces, each with its own food court and table arrangements for small groups. There was a choice of cuisine, nothing five-star, but a choice nevertheless. Wah! This was progress. Most visitors expected rows of long wooden tables moved from the dining halls, with benches on one side. The servers in veshties would go round on the other side with stainless steel buckets. Food courts! Actually, some of the older alumni were looking forward to the bone sambar, a campus special.

It was time for the mingling. The gang had agreed on a plan by which they would seek out people they had put down on a short list. They would spend no more than five minutes on pleasantries, and then steer them to a chosen spot so that the real catching up within the inner circle might begin. The trouble was the people in the short list could not be spotted. The photographic memories were useless in the sea of bald heads, flabby middles and triple chins. Thank god they had name tags, even if it meant straining to read what was written on them.

With the herding well underway the evening's conversation went at last in the desired direction, away from the dismal condition of Indian politics, the deteriorating civic sense among students today, the unending traffic jams and the appalling standard of spoken English on campus. Naturally much of the talk was about GOD, especially about exploits of the men on the sports field. And the conquests off it. Who could match Georgie as a dribbler on the football field? And Kollu's lightning fists in the boxing ring? Or the man mountain Thambi at hammer throw?

"You must be Panchu and Bajji". It was a soft voice from behind the huddle. They turned and saw a man on a wheelchair. The completely bald top was more than made up by a long, flowing beard, thick, bushy eyebrows, all silver. The smile on the face was gentle and warm. His frame was overflowing the chair, a rug covering his legs. Could it be... ? Of course, it was Thambi!

"I heard you fellows take my name, and I thought it might be you. So nice to see you all." There was the briefest moment of awkward silence, and then the group erupted in joy. All heads in all parts of the shamiana turned and added their cheers in acknowledgement.

"If you are looking for Lily, she is there" Thambi said with a wink, pointing to a section with people in classy attire and air kisses. "You won't recognize her, but what the hell, you didn't recognize me!" It was a unanimous decision that Panchu had the privilege of meeting Lily and bringing her over to the group.

Coaxing his disobedient lumbar region to assume at least a semblance of the suave gait that was once a trade mark, Panchu approached the group from a strategic tangential angle, unbuttoning his jacket so that the full length of the tie could be seen. He stopped at the edge, waiting to be recognized, to be invited to join.

Two polite glances and the group continued with its own chatter. Panchu decided to announce his presence with a cheery Hi. The circle was opened by the one nearest him and he was admitted in. The conversation in the group continued without a break. Panchu asked the gatekeeper in a loud whisper what they were discussing. It was horses, he was told. Horses? As in clip clop clip clop? Not really. It was really about the derby the previous week. Ah, the derby, the derby...

There were four women in the group. Which one was Lily? It was difficult to tell. They all had buns on top and tyres on the sides. It might be the one with the elegant Chinese collar, he thought. More like the Lily he remembered. Not wanting to take a chance he thought he would trouble the gatekeeper once more.

"Lily?"

"Lily, Economics. Lalitha Rao."

"Ah, Lalitha Rao? Lalitha Reddy. The one in the blue chiffon, there, the sleeveless blouse. That's her husband, Janak Reddy."

"Janak Reddy? You mean...?"

"Yes, the same. It's great he could take the time off to be here."

Panchu thanked his informer, took a quiet deep breath, pulled in his tummy, stuck out his chest, necktie and all, and walked up to the expansive blob of blue.

"Hi! You must be Lily!" It did not seem to register. She continued with the conversation and then noticed that the others were smiling at the newcomer in the group. She turned to acknowledge his presence.

"Hi Lily!"

"I beg your pardon..."

"Lalitha? Lalitha Rao?"

"Yes. And you are...?"

"Panchu...Pacharatnam...Physics Honours...You remember?"

"Vaguely."

She stared at his tie. Panchu was sure the memories would come flooding back. The college day dinner, the taxi ride to the soda fountain, the walk back to the girls hostel. And then she released a practiced smile...before turning back to the group and continuing with their conversation. It was Mr. Janak Reddy who asked if Panchu would care to join them. Just as he accepted the invitation and stepped in Mrs. Reddy suggested to Mr. Reddy that they really should be circulating a bit and not stay rooted there. She took him by the arm and started to step away. Panchu caught a few whispers exchanged between them. "Nice man", Panchu heard him say to Lily.

"Hmmm", and she hastened away.

"From your time?"

"Can't say", he heard her replying. "Did you see the hideous tie he was wearing?"

The rest was lost in the ambient buzz of the shamiana. Panchu recovered soon enough, only to find that the derby group had dispersed and he was all by himself.

⁂

The gang decided to make one last hop to Nair's. The rum was fine any time of year, as everybody knew. They also knew that Panchu needed just that little bit of extra attention. He could hold his liquor, but that was when he was laughing and singing. Not when glum, which was not like him. It was Gullu who suggested that they take a walk down Pulikad, even sing "Show me the way to go home" as they strolled down, just like the old days.

Mid way down Pulikad the gang opened a full throated reprise, "Wherever I may roam..." It was greeted by a light coming on in a room upstairs. They stopped. It was the same thought in all their minds...Helga. The room was exactly the same from the outside, the narrow lane leading up to the wooden door with a brass bell outside. Panchu said he would like to drop in. Just for the heck of it, he assured the others, just to see. Gullu said he would go along. No need, Panchu said. He would be right back.

The girl inside had the same inviting smile as Helga's, the same broad forehead and cheekbones. Only her skin was a shade darker and her hair a deeper brown. The two-seater, the low coffee table, the chest of drawers, they were all the same, even Jesus with the sacred heart above it. Only the turntable and stack of records was replaced with a CD player and compact speakers. Beyond the laced curtain on one side was the bed, the mosquito net down. They looked at each other across the room for a good half minute before she spoke.

"Hi, you are here for the reunion, are you not?" Another pause. "Are you Panchu?"

Before Panchu could recover from that, she added, "I am Helga's daughter"

"You are...?"

"Barbara."

"Hi Barbara."

"They call me Babli."

"How did you...?"

"Mom talks about you sometimes. She has photos of you and your friends."

"Helga, is she...?"

"She said you may be coming in for the reunion."

Just then the front door opened and shut, and a voice called out from below.

"Babli, do you have a visitor?"

The Root

Ayesha put down the diary and double checked the entries.

Monday 23
09.00am. Breakfast meeting NIOS
11.30am. Meeting editor, followed by interview with TV channel
7pm. Talk at Rotary Club

She picked up the elegant blue and yellow folder of the National Institute of Oncological Studies. The card in the slip window had her name and number in bold letters, AYESHA K RAMKUMAR R-7265. It was one of three folders handed over after her last visit. There was no need to go there as frequently any more, they had told her. Just once in six months should do, mainly for keeping tab on a few key parameters. The two other folders were bulky. They contained records of all investigations and treatments. Mr. Ramkumar had a fourth folder in his cabinet. It contained photocopies of all the bills and receipts. The originals were in his office, which had picked up the costs over two and a half years of treatment and hospitalization. And here she was, a fully recovered Ayesha, a success story from the new wave of targeted therapies. The blue and yellow folder contained a story of great drama, great suffering, great struggle and finally a great triumph.

Kiran-kaka was Senior Editor at Platform Printers & Publications. They published a very popular weekly tabloid, much respected by the better informed people of the city. The Platform had established itself very quickly, and was seeing a steady growth in readership every year. It was a vindication for Kiran, who was convinced of the need for such a tabloid, but had not seen the same enthusiasm in the proprietor family. Invited columns and spirited debates do not make circulation numbers, he was told. Who will come on board as advertisers? The trial project of a year brought in both. The circulation shot up within three months, and the advertisers were now making phone calls themselves. Project Ayesha was Kiran-kaka's idea of the year. He would sync it with the spirit of Diwali.

Kiran was also a family friend, a classmate of Ramkumarji from his schooldays, and a great admirer of Kusum-bhabi's culinary skills. He had taken charge of Ayesha's engagements from the moment the Institute confirmed with complete confidence that she had been successfully cured, and was in her own way the beacon lighting the path for scores of others. The parents were overwhelmed by the victory of medical science over a foe as fearsome as this one. They were also overcome with fatigue, and wished only to be left alone to return to a quiet life. The medical authorities, on the other hand, were insistent that the battle won was only a small step in a long drawn out war, and that the world should know about Ayesha, and join in celebrating the victory. Kiran spoke up on their behalf, and the Ramkumars went along.

Kiran Mahajan was a confirmed bachelor himself. Twenty years earlier he had been responsible for setting up the meeting between the two families to get the wild Ramkumar settle down in life.

He turned out an amiable and responsible husband after all, easily tamed by Bhabiji, who was forever grateful to Kiran for finding him for her. If she knew Kiran was visiting, she made sure he stayed back for dinner, and cooked one of his favourite dishes. Nothing fancy, no great spread, just a simple but delicious meal. Kiran would be in ecstasy over her poori-bhaji or khichdi-kadhi. The secret was in the marination of the potato. Her mother had tutored her the recipe of pahari-aloo with the curd based gravy during her very first break home after marriage. That was when she had just conceived Ayesha. Kiran-kaka was the uncontested godfather from the moment she returned home with baby Ayesha. That was the time when one part of the family had registered their disappointment with the arrival of a girl child. The Ramkumars themselves had sent out a message of steadfastness by choosing a name for her by themselves. When the name Ayesha was announced Bhabiji's family were sure she was destined to bring misfortune upon the household. They continued to call her Asha. Ram and Bhabiji were convinced she was born to be a fighter. Little did they know how soon she would prove them right.

Ayesha was now going to a gym twice a week, jogging in the park for half an hour on alternate days and had been accepted to return to the Odissi dance school. The public engagements Kiran-kaka was arranging were not the least taxing. They were done as a form of social service. She found soon enough that the audiences were more curious about what malignant tissues looked like than the bodily processes that caused them. Slide presentations of lumps were a hit. Somehow the size of a tumor always fascinated them, rather like the length of a snake seen in the backyard. Each word of mouth transmission made it just a little bit bigger. It took some tactful handling by Kiran-kaka to turn their interest to the recent breakthroughs in therapy, and her dramatic return to normal life.

⌘ ⌘ ⌘ ⌘ ⌘

Dasai had come into the Ramkumar household when the family had shifted from a tiny one-bedroom flat to a small single storeyed house in a less crowded locality. It was soon after his second promotion. The couple wished to move Ayesha to a better school. Kiran-kaka had helped in the scouting. The owners were unsure about renting it out, but were sure that if they did, it would be to people recommended by Sri. Kiran Mahajan. Dasai was walking by the house. He saw the family moving in and offered to help as a daily-wager. After two days of unpacking and settling in, it was time to send Dasai off. Bhabiji asked him to have a simple dal-roti meal before leaving. Ayesha sat with him. Over the meal Dasai explained that he was from a village in eastern UP, that there was no future for sharecropper farmers like him, and that he had been brought to the city by members of his community who lived on the outskirts. Some had landed jobs in the small factories that had come up there. Others did odd jobs as they came by their way. Could Bhabiji help? Would she know of any opening anywhere? Bhabiji asked him to return after a week. She would look out. She added an extra fifty-rupee note to his payment as he took his leave.

Ayesha guessed what was going on in her mother's mind as Dasai turned into the street and disappeared from their view. She was going to get him back.

Ramkumar agreed. They had always wanted to have a kitchen garden of their own. If they cleared the space on two sides of the house they could be growing their own vegetables. There was also the wide stretch on the terrace. If Dasai was willing, he could well become the all-rounder help in the Ramkumar household. They could make sure he earned a bit more than his daily-wager relatives. They could at least try it out for two to three months. Ayesha threw in her vote cheerfully, and the family agreed to go with the trial. It worked. After six months Ramkumar proposed that they convert the shed at the back into living quarters for Dasai, if that was acceptable to him. Dasai was now getting attached to the Ramkumar family in a way that is difficult for city folks to understand. They were pleased, of course, that Dasai consented, but we cannot say they understood. There was just a chance that Ayesha did.

The garden bloomed under Dasai's care. His green fingers were also magical. The Ramkumar family had never ever had such tasty vegetables, so good looking too. The family loved to watch Dasai as he began his morning ritual. He sat still with his palms pressed together. He raised them slowly towards the rising sun, his head following the hands. He then rose and sprinkled water from a pot in four directions, bowing each time, as if to seek permission from the soil to proceed. Only then would he turn to the family and cry out "Ram Ram!". There was one other ritual that soon became more important to the family than to Dasai himself. He always presented what he took out from the garden to Ayesha first before handing them over to Bhabiji. At times when Ayesha wasn't in, he would leave the basket below the steps. When Ayesha returned, Bhabiji would ask her to bring it into the kitchen.

⌘ ⌘ ⌘ ⌘ ⌘

When the family returned from the Institute after the tests Dasai saw that something was wrong. Ayesha went directly inside without greeting him. Bhabiji barely acknowledged his presence. Ramkumar stayed on to pay the taxi and had to face Dasai as he turned to go in. He shook his head and simply said everything would be all right. Dasai knew that it meant everything was not all right. He did not step out of the way. Ramkumar added that there was going to be an operation.

"Operation? When?"

"Soon. Very soon."

"Operation for what?"

No reply. Ramkumar rushed inside.

Who was to explain to Dasai what a malignant growth in the body was, how it was different from other boils and ulcers, and how the worst fate to descend on any person was the verdict of cancer after an examination?

When they returned from the Institute after the surgery, Dasai was better prepared. He had found out about Ayesha's condition on his own, talking to the neighbours and to the visiting doctor in Ayesha's school. It was about parts of the body connected with making a baby. Ayesha-didi would forever be childless. Worse, the beast was many-headed, and had ways to reappear in other parts of the body. He had been alerted by telephone about the family's return, and had kept lunch ready for them. He met the taxi and helped Ayesha alight. All three greeted him, although softly. They smiled. It was a smile that said that the storm had passed but the rain clouds were still thick.

At the right time. Bhabiji and Ramkumar said they would give Dasai the full picture at the right time. Some time. It was now a fortnight after Ayesha's return from the surgery. The family had decided that Ayesha would be a candidate for the new targeted therapy being offered on a limited basis to select few after surgery. She would return to the Institute very soon. Bhabiji had stepped out to the grocery when Dasai brought in the basket of vegetables. Ayesha made up her mind to tell him everything herself.

Where would she begin? How should she explain uncontrolled growth? Dasai offered an explanation himself. He said that some things are grown by man's design. Some things grow paying no heed to man. Yes, that's true, said Ayesha, sensing a useful opening. Dasai asked Ayesha if she had ever wondered where potatoes came from. She had no idea. He took her at once to the small potato patch at the side and opened up the soil so she could look underneath. He explained to her that the cluster of bulbs there was really an uncontrolled growth of the same root. Nobody can say how many bulbs there will be, and when they will stop growing. So true, agreed Ayesha.

But the bulbs that grow from the potato root are healthy. They serve a useful purpose. Dasai was quick to catch on. Can there be uncontrolled growth that is unhealthy? Ah, that would be a problem, would it not? We see that in the garden too. There are many plants that live off other plants and trees, eating them up and killing them in the end. Ayesha's lesson plan was quite redundant now. She was learning as much from Dasai as he was from her. One last idea remained. She would need special preparation for that. Ayesha excused herself, promising that they would continue the chat the next day.

Kiran-kaka joined them for dinner that evening. He wanted to walk the Ramkumars through the entire process of the new targeted therapy that they were signing up for. He had some up to date information that he wanted to share with them. Ayesha entered the room and immediately asked him if he knew where potatoes came from. And she reported her entire conversation with Dasai that afternoon. The parents were surprised, but not annoyed. Kiran-kaka was thrilled. He realized at once the potential of Ayesha becoming the Ambassador of hope for cancer.

Ayesha had a question for Kiran-kaka. It was her search for a simple way to explain cancerous growth within a single human body, but not across two or more humans.

"You mean like a contagious disease? Spreading from person to person?"

"Yes. Why does it only remain within a single person? Why won't my cancer get transferred to Amma or Papa? Or to you?"

Kiran-kaka caught on instantly. She was struggling with an incomplete understanding of systems and system properties. The idea of a system's functions and dysfunctions had to be understood with system boundaries defined. It was good to see Ayesha switched on, but this was no time to get diverted to that.

The aroma drifting in from the kitchen decided that he would take her on, but it would be an entire session in itself. He would also get her to read something. He agreed that Ayesha's question was the right springboard for exploration of the frontiers.

Dasai took his place at the lower step. Seated at the top step Ayesha began with the same question.

"Dasai-bhaiya, I have a question for you today. Why is uncontrolled growth only within a single body, and not passed on to another body?"

"You mean...Why does it happen only within one potato plant? Why doesn't a potato plant become two potato plants? Then four, then eight, and then sixteen?"

"Yes. Something like that."

"It happens in the planting season, does it not?"

"When you want it to happen. When you do the planting. Not by itself."

"Ah, yes...Not by itself. But what if I did something from the outside that made it happen by itself?" What if I put something inside the plant...From the outside...And the inside went on and made it happen by itself?"

Ayesha gasped. Was that possible? Seeing her staring ahead, Dasai asked softly, "Ayesha-didi...?"

Was that possible, Ayesha asked. Has he seen it happen?

Dasai confessed he had not seen anything like that himself, but it did seem possible, did it not? How else can you explain the hundreds of chickens being turned out day after day on the chicken farms? They all look the same, they all behave the same way. And they are all tasteless the same way.

Ayesha noted the question flashing before her. Could there be good cancer and bad cancer? Like good cholesterol and bad cholesterol? Her mind was now racing. She thought about words and their meanings. There were simple and straight forward meanings for words. There were also hidden meanings that suggested something more, usually something unwanted. Wasn't cancer like that? Evil, ruthless, cruel... There seemed no other way of looking at cancer. Like Ravana. Always a villain. Was he really a villain? Or Rakshasa. She remembered how in her childhood she dreaded encountering a rakshsha walking back at night from her friend's home. Much later she read about good rakshasas, doing what they were destined to do, even married by god-like figures in the scriptures. She felt relieved, but the unintended meaning remained.

Dasai agreed. He never despised a rakshasa. In their village shrines there was a place for rakshasa characters. He offered an explanation. If cancer was given to us by nature, then there must be a place for it in nature. It must be serving some purpose of nature. Ayesha could not help being drawn to Dasai's words. And yet, she could not deny the struggle within her to come to terms with other ways of looking at cancer.

Dasai wanted to continue.

"Oh, one more thing. Why do we have so many crores of people hungry in this world? Can't we take the god of cancer on our side and create bountiful harvests and have an abundance of foodgrains?"

"Dasai-bhaiya, if anybody can grow enough food to feed the world, it is you!"

"No, no, didi. It is people like you. Educated people like you. If I had a son, I would send him to school and college to study like you. Who knows, maybe with god's grace, he would find a way to do it."

"But you have magic in your fingers, Dasai-bhaiya!"

The therapeutic process appeared surprisingly uncomplicated to Ayesha and her parents. They knew, of course, that the complexity was in the technology being employed, the precision needed in identifying the targets, isolating them and then bringing them down. There was continuous observation and assessment. All of this was with a sophistication not seen or heard of before. It was certainly way beyond fixing the fracture after Ayesha's cycling spill.

When they reached home after the first round of treatment it was known that there would be periodic visits to the Institute over the next three to six months. The home routine changed completely. The dining room chatter dropped to whispered conversations. Dasai went about his work without coming in their way.

On the day of the last visit to the Institute, there was an atmosphere of relief and joy in the Ramkumar home. There was every chance that the specialists at the Institute would give Ayesha the final clean chit. After her puja Bhabiji put on the sari that her mother had given her on her return home with Ayesha. Ramkumar played the family's favourite picnic music on the CD player. He sent word for Dasai to join them in seeking goddess Lakshmi's blessing before setting out.

Dasai came in beaming. He was carrying two large baskets, the size of the hen coop chairs in the veranda, one in either hand, barely managing their weight as he came up the steps. He set the baskets down and opened the covers. The baskets were full of potatoes. There must have been hundreds of them. They were freshly harvested, unwashed and still smelled of the earth. They were all egg shaped, identical in size. Dasai was still beaming as he bowed and greeted the family. Ram Ram.

[Cancer survivors often have insights and learnings that do not occur to others. The play 'Monsters in the Dark' led to the opening of our eyes and ears.]

The Soil

It was one of the most cherished traditions in the Lal family. At least three generations that had gathered in the living room after the Diwali lunch agreed that it was started by Sriman Uttam Kumar Lal a year or two before his retirement. Uttamji was Deputy Postmaster overseeing the Eastern Region of the area then known as United Provinces. The acronym UP remained for Uttar Pradesh after the reorganization of states in independent India.

Uttamji's predecessor in the Post & Telegraph Department was an Englishman who owned a Zeiss Ikon bellows camera. It had a study dark brown leather case, probably made of Indian buffalo hide, which had survived many field trips over many Indian summers. On handing over charge to Uttamji the saheb also presented the camera to him. With the camera came eight rolls of size 120 film, with expiry dates well after two years. At that time the price of a roll of film in the Civil Lines photo studio was about the same as getting two poplin shirts stitched. The first roll was loaded at the farewell tea itself, and three group pictures were taken. The remaining five were taken in the small garden in the bungalow, with combinations of family members filling the frame. Uttamji must have got it right. Only one frame had an under-exposure and one had a shake. That left six good pictures out of eight frames. Not a bad score for a first attempt. Some said that it was the magic of Zeiss Ikon, you couldn't go wrong with it. Others said it was Uttamji, he was a natural. A week later it was Diwali, and the entire family of uncles, aunts and cousins got to see the pictures. Within a year a family album had been created. The seven other rolls were used up in that period. Album volumes were added year to year and the dates painted in white with a thin brush on the top right hand corner of the covers. Uttamji was giving up on new clothes at Holi and Diwali festivals and buying roll films instead. In a few years, even before Uttamji was called away to his heavenly abode, it became the custom on Diwali day to gather around the family albums.

⌘ ⌘ ⌘ ⌘ ⌘

Nobody used a camera anymore. Many in the family had never seen one. There were no printed photographs either. The Lal family went to great lengths to create printed images and put them into specially fabricated albums. It cost a fortune, but it was a Lal tradition. Two photographs from an earlier generation were great hits Diwali after Diwali. One was that of a 1953 Morris Oxford sedan, said to be the progenitor of the Indian automobile industry. The other was a Webley & Scott revolver. Nobody had seen real automobiles and guns except in the public museums. Private ownership of these had been prohibited since the last forty years. A century ago even Uttamji's father had probably never seen a camera, certainly never held one in his hands. It was Uttamji who brought one into the Lal home. The prized Zeiss Ikon was now preserved in an air tight cubical clear acrylic container, which was placed prominently in the centre shelf of the display in the living room, the leather case by its side. There were other relics and souvenirs from the years just before and after Independence on two shelves. The rest of the space was taken by trophies won by the current generation.

On a small table in front of the display was the latest addition. It was a shiny pyramid of stainless steel, matt finished, about 15 inches high. It was a rolling trophy that young Pranav had won in a Maths Olympiad. The engraving faced the room: Pranav Lal 2060. The label below the camera in the middle shelf said it was a hundred and twenty five years ago that Uttamji had received the camera from his angrez boss.

Pranav's proficiency in Math was because of another New Dawn initiative, the Numero Systems Immersion programme. It was one of four such Immersion thrusts for fast track acquisition of skills without conventional classroom instruction. The Immersions required an alternative literacy, a high imaging fluency, and bypassed reading and writing proficiency. It had been proven amply that the three Rs of olden times actually hampered true learning. The three other Immersion thrusts were Expressive Aesthetics, Ideation History and Meta-civics. These were sometimes called the four pillars of the New Dawn mansion of learning. The editor of Alpha Bulletin, the newsletter of the most prestigious society of conventional mathematics based in the island society once known as the United Kingdom, wished to interview Pranav and sent him a list of twenty questions. Pranav struggled to answer the questions, confessing he could not read or write fluently enough. It was enough to convince Alpha that the Immersion programme was a fraud. Pranav sent his replies anyway. It was in the imaging language that was more suitable for grappling several complex streams of logic simultaneously. Alpha confessed that they did not have the required fluency in the language used and sought his permission to write about him in the newsletter without the interview.

Pranav was one half of the pair born to Rukmini and Rajat. Most couples opted for the two-children plan offered by the National Health Commission. Some stayed with a single child. Many chose not to have any. The incentives attached were progressively scaled. They were attractive and genuine. They worked. Rukmini and Rajat themselves were from two-children homes. They were the first generation products of the plan introduced in the year the country had successfully implemented the New Dawn Family Health policy and stabilized the country's population at 1.3 billion. The best part of the plan was that a couple choosing to be conservative and opting for a pair could have them both together and be done with parenting in one conception. It could be any gender combination. Not surprisingly, most chose to have one boy and one girl. Gender choice was available even for the couples choosing to have only one child. Dadiji recalled in amusement, not without a hint of anger, how in their child bearing years there was the dreaded sex determination test that pregnant women were subjected to, and the ingenious ways in which the husband's family despatched the female baby. It was all beyond the comprehension of the current generation. The sex ratio had been a healthy 98:102 for the last two census tallies. It was in favour of women, as if making up for the sins of past generations.

New Dawn was the brand that was attached to many social development programmes introduced by the upstart political party that called itself the Truth Alone Party, popularly called TAP. Members of the party were called Taps. TAP faced objections from the grand old parties of the past when it first announced itself as Satyameva Party. The matter went to court.

They replied that since no other party had upheld the motto inscribed under the national emblem, what could possibly be the objection to their standing up for it. The Supreme Court quashed the objections, and the name remained. The party's counter-argument won over the people instantly.

The party made its presence felt in 2019, as a regional force and a strong presence in the opposition at the centre. By 2024 they had arrived on the national stage. They did that with their steadfast adherence to truth, calling an axe an axe. The truth was that many unquestioned and destructive practices in society needed the axe. The party had a truth over the truths, which was to give every citizen of the land access to the axe. In the early years the skeptics had said that all the intellectualizing TAP indulged in might work in the South, where the party had its origins, but would it work in, say, UP? The truth is that it did. Take the city of Kanpur, where the Lal khandan resided.

The New Dawn Integrated Urban Planning programme had not only arrested the unchecked growth of the city, but had created three concentric rings of commodities production that was carried out at the scale of an industrial conglomerate. The production centres took what Kanpur city discarded and gave back Kanpur city what it wanted. The city was self-sufficient in meeting most of its needs. The first ring was devoted to recycling the city's waste into basic raw materials that the second ring would use for conversion into usable materials. This included organically rich soil and nutrients for vegetable and grain production in the second ring. The third ring was reserved for the production of non-consumable goods made from the recycled materials that had markets beyond Kanpur city – from linen and garments, through household furniture, to solar powered personal transport. The slogan was "If it works in UP, it will work anywhere". Kanpur became the flag bearing benchmark for integrated urban planning everywhere.

The programme amply demonstrated what TAP had offered people as a dream at the start: communal harmony through the achievement of living harmony. Petty religious rituals leading to violent clashes were only historical oddities. Whatever might be the community identities suggested by the surnames, or festivals such as Diwali, people went by the social practices introduced by New Dawn, rather than cling to rituals that served little purpose.

Nowhere was this more clearly seen than in the matter of deaths in a family. First, New Dawn had succeeded in getting the population to completely reject the ancient practice of prolonging life. Medical Science was oriented to the achievement of a full and productive three-score-and-ten years of life, rather than abetting invasions on the body through a narrow and rather flawed interpretation of the Hippocratic oath. It was now possible for a person to choose the age and date of one's departure within the prescribed limit of 75 years, and every registered medical establishment was obliged to help the person fulfil the wish. Organ donations on death were redundant. There were no crematoria or cemeteries within the city anymore. With past burials of most communities at a depth of six feet under the ground, the new programme had shifted ten feet of soil from all burial grounds, completely intact, to the first of the three rings around the city.

This part of the ring was about one-fourth of the perimeter, and formed an arc, rising to a height of over a hundred meters. It had multiple levels of the compost storage, neatly stacked and classified by family origin. More recent departures had a more humane and sound bioprocessing technology for conversion before transfer to the outer rings of the city. Once the date of departure was chosen the medical establishment gave the person a calibrated and highly customized transcranial radiation for what people of Uttamji's generation would call the last journey. Transportation was arranged to a specially designated spot at Sunset Point at the edge of the city. All good-byes were celebratory in nature, and just before the transport was boarded. Nobody accompanied the person to Sunset Point. An hour's meditation in complete peace, and it was over. The body was taken over by a common metropolitan facility for processing. It was aptly called The Higher Purpose. The richest soil nutrients came from The Higher Purpose.

An especially attractive feature of the food production centres all around the city was the satisfaction people had from the personalized attention it offered. Your family would get fresh, tasty, organically produced potatoes from the waste you had yourself contributed to the centre.

⌘ ⌘ ⌘ ⌘ ⌘

Rajat Lal, like all others, made a personal trip to the suppliers in the outer rings only once or twice a year, for special occasions. All routine household supply, including all foodstuff, was at the doorstep through the extensive underground network of chutes. There was one receiving terminal every kilometer, from where a robotized cart delivered the goods home. It was Diwali again, and the personalized service for essential groceries for the family feast was to be hand-picked by Rajat.

Rajat reached the Centre for Family Reunion. He ran the tip of his forefinger along the edge of the visor strapped to his forehead. It was to double check the groceries list. The icons flashed before him and rolled by, confirming the order that had been placed. He stepped in. The Floor Manager was expecting Rajat.

"Malati Lal?" Rajat nodded in acknowledgement.

"Your mother?"

"Yes." Rajat felt a sense of family pride swelling within.

"The Lal plot has given us an exceptional yield this month."

"That is good to hear."

"It must be because the soil knew you were coming." He winked, and added, "It's known to happen sometimes."

"Perhaps", Rajat replied with a smile.

The Manager excused himself for a moment to reach up to a shelf for a violet coloured self-cooling carton marked with a hologram of his mother.

"Violet was her favourite colour, we see." Rajat nodded in agreement, feeling an eagerness overtaking him.

"I see that you have asked for bharta baingan – ten pieces. Diwali lunch?"

"Yes, we remember her on Diwali. She was very fond of bharta."

"Family reunions at Diwali are what keep us going. When they get together it is a bharta in itself! My best regards to your family!"

Rajat thanked the Manager as he looked over the twelve baingan in the carton, identical in shape and size, The two extra pieces were with the compliments of the Centre for the special occasion. The Manager kept the carton aside and assured Rajat it would be at his doorstep even before he reached home.

⁂ ⁂ ⁂ ⁂ ⁂

The Lal khandan gathered around the family albums after the traditional Diwali lunch. Rajat announced that this Diwali they would begin with an album he had specially created on his mother, Malatiji. It was her one hundredth birth anniversary year.

The Temp

It was his first day at the office. He was at the lift 5 minutes before 9 o'clock. While the lift was on its way down a pretty young girl joined him and started a conversation.

"Hi! You must be Bhushan sir."

"Hello. Yes, I am Bhushan Prabhakar. Are you... ?"

"Yes, I am part of AstraTech. My name is Bela, Bela Mehta."

"Hi Bela."

"I am to show you around today. But you almost got there before me!"

"Old habit... "

"Are you always so punctual? We'll all have to shape up then!"

They got into the lift. There were six others. A funeral silence took over the lift compartment as it made its way up to the sixteenth floor. People resumed their conversations the moment they stepped out. Bela introduced Bhushan to Kitty, the receptionist, and led him to his desk. They were among the first to get there. Two minutes ahead. Two minutes after nine it was not much different. Bhushan asked when people usually got in. Around nine twenty-five, Bela said. The boss got in at nine thirty. But she would start him on his induction straight away. Item 1. The coffee corner. A good place to start.

Bela was curious. What was a retired silver haired gentleman of sixty-five doing there as a Temp? He pressed the Cappuccino button and spoke without looking up. It was about cyber security. Ah, that. But the Company already had double firewalls and the best anti-malware systems in place. He would explain, he said, perhaps over lunch. It went beyond systems protecting the computers.

The next three hours were pleasantly spent, with Bela introducing Bhushan to the Programme Heads and their teams in their colour coded spaces. Most had the same question. Bela replied most of them. The boss, known variously as Ashok sir or AD or Chief or simply Boss, welcomed him with a corporate hug and offered coffee. Seeing Bela by his side he commented that he might already have had a cup or two by then. They moved on. She was now very protective, treating Bhushan like her father. By a half past twelve Bhushan's computer connection was up and running, and his desk had everything he could ever ask for. Bela said she would leave him to himself for a while and pick him up at a quarter past one for lunch. They could chat then. Would there be a quiet corner? She could arrange it.

By the third day the morning routine had been well set. Bhushan had more time by himself at his desk. Bela picked him at lunch time. The promised chat had not taken place. Bela thought it best to let it take its time. The boss had said something about an internal seminar by Bhushan. They stepped out sometimes for a bite. There were at least four good eateries nearby with comfortable seating. They preferred the one which served pav bhaji.

⁂

The internal seminar was scheduled at 5.00. People could wind up early and stay longer if there was more interest in the subject. It was titled 'STAYING AHEAD' and sub-titled 'the era of cyber warfare'. The topic excited the entire staff. There was room in the seminar hall for only a hundred. Live streaming was set up at four other meeting areas. No recording was permitted. All cellphones were left at the work stations. It was not going to be possible to replay the talk. The seminar was announced a fortnight earlier. People adjusted their out of office work to be there.

Bhushan said he would begin with two stories. The first was about the crash of an Indian Air Force fighter jet in the Northeast two years earlier. After a front page mention a day after the crash there was no further reporting in the media. There was consistent stonewalling of questions raised in the Parliament. A week later a private ethical hacker revealed how it might have been a cyber attack on the aircraft system by a 'hostile neighbour' to teach India a lesson. It also showed how vulnerable the Air Force was to such attacks. The second story was from Albania. Customers at one of the country's biggest banks got a shock when a curt text popped up on their cellphones: "Your account has been blocked. The balance of your account is zero. Thank you." The message was shown to be fake, but the damage had been done. There was panic in the financial markets and most trade came to a standstill. The source of the cyber attack was traced to a country with a long history of cyber terrorism. While some called it a mischief attack, to demonstrate what was possible, the government statement was that the assaults were "absolutely the same as a conventional military aggression, only by other means."

At this point Bhushan was ten minutes into the seminar. He looked into his watch and said that in a minute it would be ten minutes past five. He urged the audience to open their laptops and boot up. They found that at 5.05 all of them had sent a 'get well soon' message to Ashok sir, the boss. At 5.06 they had all received a thank you reply. It was all done by Bhushan, of course, to show how easy it is to hack into office computer systems. Most in the audience laughed. Some were worried. It did not stop there. Bhushan asked Ashok sir to keep his system on just a moment longer. It was projected on to the seminar screen. Bhushan pressed a few keys on his laptop to activate a command. The audience saw to its horror a message appearing on the screen. It was from Ashok sir to the CFO, requesting action to offload 40 percent shares to a hostile buyer and then file for bankruptcy. The CFO was present in the seminar. He confirmed that the message had arrived on his computer. Bhushan keyed in a command again. The seminar screen and the CFO's computer had the message, HAPPY FATHER'S DAY! Within moments all screens went blank. There was the expected panic in the room. Bhushan requested everybody to simply reboot. Everything was back to normal. It was merely a demo.

Bhushan chided the audience for their blind reliance on the Company's anti-virus programme and the ten-character passwords. It was simply not enough. If an enemy wished to break through them it could be done in two weeks – as he had done. He then introduced the topic of the seminar: the need for multiple layers of protection in a multi-dimensional cyberspace. The best part of that space was its darkness. The seminar ended with a conundrum posed to the audience, which he said had remained unsolved over thousands of years. How do we keep a secret, secret?

As everybody rushed to their work stations to collect their cellphones, the boss took Bhushan and Bela aside to ask if they would like to join him for a drink and a bite. They could meet at the lobby at a quarter past seven. Bhushan stayed back to pack up. His cell phone beeped. He looked down the corridor to see if anybody was there. He sat down to take the call. After a few moments he rose and closed the door to the room. The chat groups in the Company fired up. They were abuzz with reactions to the seminar. A common thread in all of them was the question: could Bhushan be trusted with the Company's cybersecurity?

The boss met Bela at the lobby on the dot at 7.15. Bhushan had not arrived. They waited. Ten minutes later Bela went to the security desk and asked them to call the sixteenth floor for Bhushan. She was told that he had left the building. Checking his system the security supervisor confirmed that he had stepped out five minutes before seven. There were three men who had come in asking for him. Bhushan sir had left with them. They took him to a car waiting outside.

Bhushan was sandwiched between two men on the back seat. The third was at the wheel. As soon as the car turned the corner one of the men slipped a hood over Bhushan's head and covered him in a shawl. In about thirty minutes it was quieter outside. The car picked up speed. Bhushan realized they were heading out of the city.

⌘ ⌘ ⌘ ⌘ ⌘

The boss and Bela decided to take a chance and go to Bhushan's home. They had the address. It was a narrow lane off the approach street. They had to leave the car there and walk. There were small shops on both sides of the lane. There were ironmongers, shops selling second hand hardware and electrical basics, chicken and eggs, a mutton stall, two pawn shops, a gas welder, a two wheeler repair shop and a scrap dealer. People lived above the shops. Bela went to the pawn shop that was given as a landmark and asked about Bhushan. He lived upstairs, she was told. The pawnbroker owned the rooms. Was there anybody there? No, Bhushan babu lived by himself. It was about this time he returned in the evening. He guessed that the lady and the saheb were from the office. Would they like to wait upstairs? He had the key. The small door next to the pawnbroker shop could easily be missed. It had two men seated in front, smoking. The pawnbroker shooed them away. A heavy chain connecting the two narrow doors had a padlock on it. It was opened for the Boss and Bela, and they went up a wooden staircase that was narrow and steep, with a rope on one side for support. It was dark. The pawnbroker led them up and switched on a lamp at the head of the stairs. He asked them to go inside and make themselves comfortable. He would arrange some chai for them.

Bhushan's home was a single long passage, like a railway bogie, divided into three sections. There were first the living and bedroom sections, followed by a dining table and four chairs at the far end. One side of the dining area was a small kitchen. It was neat, clean and orderly. There was a partition door that presumably led to a bathroom. The living area was crowded. Most of the floor and two walls were covered with old, ornate objects that made it look like an antique shop. As they were looking at the collection with fascination a clock chimed. They turned to see a wall clock of traditional design, beautifully crafted. It had an engraved brass pendulum. There were two brass cylinders with delicate chains that served as the winding mechanism. The casing was polished rosewood, with an elegant carved head. Each of the hour marks had a gold stud on the outer ring. There were goblets on stands, brass trays and plaques, porcelain crafts and carpets piled on the floor, all of it giving the room an Arabian air. With only one light on at the entrance the atmosphere was entrancing. They chose to wait without switching on any other light. They waited half an hour, with chances of Bhushan's arrival diminishing by the minute. They decided to call it a day and informed the pawnbroker they were leaving. They gave their names to him, requesting him to let Bhushan know.

⌘ ⌘ ⌘ ⌘ ⌘

The two men stood Bhushan before a large table, standing either side of him. It was a large warehouse, with packaged goods stored in racks up to the ceiling, which looked at least forty feet high. There was a wide passage in the middle from one end to the other. The table was at the end near the entrance. The sliding door had been shut. There was nobody else in the warehouse. The third man, the driver, was standing at the far end. They took off the hood. One of them patted Bhushan's back and said someone had to speak first. Bhushan protested, finding his voice, sounding like a Jeep engine just come to life. The second man asked politely who it was speaking to them.

"You know who. I'm Bhushan."

"Bhushan who?"

"Prabhakar. Bhushan Prabhakar. AstraTech. You asked for me at the ground floor reception. I don't know who you are."

"I am Jeevan. You can call me Jeev. And this is Jonathan, called Jon. And you are... Bhushan Prabhakar?"

Before Bhushan could reply, the one called Jon had yanked his silver haired wig off, revealing a bald pate with a barely visible band of hair all around. He grinned widely, waiting for protests. Bhushan was left speechless. Jeev was helpful.

"Lost for words, Mr. Akshat Narula? A memory lapse? Here, please sit down. Drink some water. Let's see if we can help you recover."

Jeev drew up a chair for Bhushan before the table and placed a bottle of water before him. He and Jon continued standing. Bhushan pushed the bottle away, leaned back and stared ahead. He mumbled.

" What do you want from me? I am just..."

"A cybersecurity consultant at AstraTech, is that right?"

"A software engineer with a special interest in..."

"A man of many talents. In much demand."

Jon dug into the large pocket of his cargo pants and pulled out a handful of spent cartridges. He dropped them on the table before Bhushan. Jeev picked them up one by one and stood them in a line before Bhushan. His free hand was on Bhushan's shoulder once again.

"Four spent shells... thirty-o-six... the dream rifle, every true marksman longed to own one... once upon a time... when hunting was not a sin and you could serve your guests fresh deer meet from your own kill... with a scope mounted you could drop the animal from five hundred yards with one shot... or a human..."

He paused, waiting for a reaction. Bhushan knocked down the upright shells and looked away. Jeev picked up one of the shells and turned the rim towards Bhushan's face.

"Hmmm... What does it say here? P-O-F... What does that mean? Jon, what do you think POF means?"

"POF? Maybe Akshat sir can tell us."

Pakistan Ordnance Factory. Large quantities of ammunition were routinely smuggled out, with insiders working hand-in-glove with agents of the black market. The thirty caliber rifle ammunition was the most abundant in production and the most in demand. Naturally a lot of it crossed the borders to reach eager buyers everywhere. Akshat was one among many. Jon pulled out the original polypropylene box for packing cartridges. He placed it before Bhushan and opened the lid. There were five empty slots.

"Aahh, perhaps Akshat sir's memory is coming back now..."

"He may recall what happened to the fifth shell. Was it fired? Did it remain unused?"

There was no escape. Bhushan was compelled to reply. He could not say exactly how many rounds were fired. It was a long time ago. It was another time... another life. He never counted. He never collected spent shells. Why bring up that now? He gave it all up long ago. Jeev thanked him for speaking up. He added that Akshat, alias Bhushan, might have given up the past, but the past had not given him up. He signaled to Jon, who walked to a rack on the left and picked up a large sized carton. It had markings on the side that said it was a set of golf clubs. He opened the carton and took out a polished wooden case with brass hinges and a brass handle in front. He laid the case on the table and opened it. It was a Springfield rifle, 30-06, bolt action, with a clip magazine for five rounds. Above the rifle was a telescopic sight. On one side were two extra clip magazines and a muzzle silencer. They were all implanted neatly in a base with deep red velvet lining.

Jon showed Bhushan that the rifle was loaded. He waved to the third man at the far end, who uncovered a standing target and moved away to one side. Jon handed Bhushan the rifle and asked him to test himself. He could remain seated to steady his arms. Jeev and Jon took out their pistols and held them pointed at Bhushan.

Bhushan took his time. He pressed his palms together and bowed to the rifle. He picked it up slowly and caressed the rifle stock with his left hand and the butt with his cheek. He closed his eyes with the rifle in position, the barrel lowered. He opened his eyes and raised the barrel slowly, shifting his shoulder and back, settling into a steady breath. He closed one eye.

Five out of five within an inch. Wahwahi! Jeev patted Bhushan warmly as Jon took away the rifle. They drew up two more chairs and sat across the table facing Bhushan.

"You have not lost touch."

"It is all in the past. I have put it behind me."

"Muscle memory I suppose. You can never really put it behind."

"I retired long ago. I only do advisory work in cybersecurity."

"And you do a bloody good job too. Why? Because you know the world of cybercrime inside out."

"I don't want to go back..."

"Your talent is needed. It cannot be allowed to be wasted."

Bhushan buried his head in his arms on the table. There was the faintest trace of a sob. The men waited patiently. Jeev leaned across and spoke softly. He assured Bhushan that nobody need know about the past... about the last job... the four spent shells from the last rounds fired. Bhushan looked up. Jeev continued and said they knew where the fifth round was fired. In fact they had the fifth empty shell. Jon took it out and placed it on the table before Bhushan. Nobody need know about that last shot. It was Bhushan's personal target. Only three men had the full story... the evidence... Jeev, Jon and Ustad DG sir. Akshat saheb would remember DG sir, of course.

⌘ ⌘ ⌘ ⌘ ⌘

With Bhushan not appearing at the office the next two days Ashok sir and Bela thought it was time to do something. Anything but informing the police station. Ashok sir sought an appointment with a college mate who was till recently the Commissioner and had been transferred to the CBI. Mr. Digvijay "Diggy" Singh, IPS, had kept in touch through Diwali and New Year greetings. They met at the Club. Diggy Singh promised to put someone on the job. A week later they met again. Singh sahib had something to report.

Bhusan Prabhakar had many aliases. He had at least five Aadhar cards, as many cellphones, and had taken tenement flats in widely separated parts of the city. His stated occupations were diverse too. Interestingly each of the flats had unique interiors. One of them was all around ghazals and thumris. Another had loads of science fiction stuff. There was reason to believe that all this was necessary for him to practice his main occupation. Bhushan was a marksman. His services were sought both in covert police operations and in high stakes criminal operations. In at least two cases, not surprisingly, the two had worked hand in hand. In the two neighbouring states of Maharashtra and Gujarat the marked increase in police encounter deaths had a strikingly common pattern. The fatal shots were fired not from police weapons, but a high powered rifle a short distance from the site. An abandoned brick kiln, a water tank, parked railway wagons... There was a sudden end to the third party shootings. Bhushan was missing. He was either on the run from a party he had let down or had given up his trade. There was no evidence of his owning any firearms himself in any of the places lived. The rifle used would be sophisticated and very expensive. It must have been arranged for each job taken on. It was increasingly clear that he was abducted. That did not look good. Singh saheb's men would continue the investigation. Yes, it would be off the record. For now.

Ten days had passed already. Ashok sir and Bela met over coffee to talk about next steps. They had to make some sort of announcement to the staff. Something short and non-committal, not attracting too much attention. Bela said she would prepare a draft and share it with him. Ashok sir's phone beeped. It was Diggy Singh. He had news, but he would keep it short for now. First, the dreaded mafia boss Ustad had been killed. He had plunged down the middle stream of the Jog Falls. They suspected suicide. The investigating party found the body downstream. It had a bullet hole at the left temple. A trade mark sniper shot. Three days later they found a partly decomposed body a mile from the Forest Office. It was in a shallow pit covered with building rubble and moldy leaves. The body was riddled with about fifteen bullets. Singh saheb signed off.

Ashok sir asked Bela to draft the announcement with great care. She switched on her laptop. The screen turned bright and colourful. A greeting zoomed in: HAPPY FATHER'S DAY! The cellphone rang. It was Ashok sir, saying he had just received a Father's Day greeting. Both the screens turned blank at the same time.

The Clubhouse

The two families were the closest friends. They visited each other at least once a week, spent evenings at the cinema together, went on holidays together, borrowed freely from each other's kitchens and looked after each other's homes when either family went to its home town. The children spending nights together was standard practice. They had extra durries and mattresses kept ready all the time. They had their favourite razais too. It was no surprise then that the Rao and Murthy families named the children the same. There were two boys by the name of Raghavendra and two girls named Gitanjali. Was there confusion about that when they got together? It was never a problem. One had the nick name Raghu, the other was Raghav. The girls were Gitu and Anju. Ah, yes, it did cause some amusement when they travelled together by train and the full names were given for reservations. Also when the two girls visited the dentist together.

The Rao home had a secret clubhouse in one corner of the garden under a guava tree. Only one outsider was given membership. That was Dodo, the Rao family dog. Dodo also served as the President of the Club by day and the watchdog of the club after sunset. He was happier there than inside the house. There was a password to enter.

The password changed on the first of every month. It was Come-Dodo-Go-Dodo when they started. It was Here-Dodo-There-Dodo once, and Andar-Dodo-Bahar- Dodo another time. The clubhouse at the Murthy home was the attic above the children's bedroom. It was called The Gufa. If the Raos took Dodo along while visiting the Murthys, which was often, he would run directly upstairs, take the wooden steps up to the attic and park himself there. When the children stomped their way up, singing in unison, they would call out the password to Dodo and he would let them in.

The families never lost contact, not even when they relocated to different cities, one of them to another country. They would always say that their best times were in the lovely old Allahabad. They even had a reunion holiday together in Allahabad. They did a picnic in Khusro Bagh, and made sure the hamper included the incomparable safeda guavavs. They took a boat ride along the Sangam, walked down Civil Lines for a chaat, and took in a movie at the only cinema house still standing. Anand Bhavan was closed to the public, but they managed to persuade the young chowkidar, the son of the old chowkidar, to let them walk in the garden for a few minutes. A drive to the University campus and around the old cathedral was mandatory. It was the route the school bus took every day to the little town of Prayag, five miles from central Allahabad. Next to the railway station of Prayag was the abandoned site of Annie Besant School. There was a funeral atmosphere when the two families stood in silence next to the few crumbling walls that remained.

But the sound of happy children alighting from the school bus was all around them. The four children remembered the songs they sang on arrival. They found themselves humming one together.

The next day the two families went to Naini to pay homage to Raghav's grandfather. He had been incarcerated in the Central Prison there along with a large number of freedom fighters. Jawaharlal Nehru, Gobind Ballabh Pant and Feroze Gandhi were among them. On the way back they stopped at the two-storied house from where the fathers had watched Nehru drive back after his release from prison. The street was deserted, but the fathers recounted the occasion in great detail.

At that time it was just the two young men and their wives. The children had not arrived.

The townsfolk of Allahabad were all out on the streets. It was an air of jubilation. It was late at night too. The young Raos and Murthys drove to a street where the old box model Ford could be parked to a side and then walked down to where the people had gathered. As the narrow lane opened up to the main road, it was all colour, all noise, and all senses were awakened. There were impromptu bands assembled here and there, groups shouting slogans in chorus, hordes thronging the road and all the balconies on both sides, and all the rooftops. They were singing, waving flags, distributing sweets. The painted banners had the familiar smiling face of Jawaharlal Nehru, Panditji to all. Some banners had Gandhi thrown in for good measure. It looked like a gathering at a wedding to which the whole of Allahabad had been invited. Everybody seemed very happy about something, but not quite paying attention to it. The families made their way to the first floor balcony of a home that had reserved the space for them. The night was endless, nobody was in a hurry to get home. And then...a roar of jubilant voices was heard at one end of the road, sweeping down in waves towards the spot they had occupied. The moment had arrived. In the distance they could see a large convertible car, the top opened, cruising down at walking pace, as if it was a baarat carrying a bridegroom, petromax lanterns on either side, flowers tossed on it from all sides. He was free. He was going home. Standing in the car, smiling, hands pressed together in namaskar was the man himself, the one they were all talking about, the man who should be the leader of the nation awaiting its rebirth.

Aahh...Allahabad. Al-a-bad to the angrez-oiented, Ilahabad to the locals. Allahabad on the railway platform. Abad of the supreme being, abode of the peaceful, city of the joyful, city of learning, city of culture. The confluence of rivers was aptly symbolic of the many more confluences in the city. If it was not for the demands of their professions the two families might have made their permanent residences in the tranquil Allahabad.

The Rao family went to Manchester when he had an assignment in a large bio-technology project. It had two extensions. The family stayed then back.

They made England their home. Raghu and Gitu fitted in easily, going to the University and getting the jobs they wanted. The Murthys stayed in India, but moved to Delhi, taking a flat in Ghaziabad. It was Delhi, but also not Delhi, Ghaziabad shown in maps as a city in Uttar Pradesh. Raghav was in Quality Assurance in a software services company with clients mostly in Europe. Anju was a Research Associate in the Department of History in the University. She loved her job.

⌘ ⌘ ⌘ ⌘ ⌘

One day Raghav found himself in police custody in a station house in Ghaziabad. It happened very fast, with Raghav totally unprepared for it. It went into the statistics of the state police force. They were building up an image of a force acting fast.

On his way home from work he stopped his motorcycle at a traffic signal and waited for it to turn green. A second two-wheeler weaved between vehicles, screeched to a halt, lost control and hit a cyclist waiting in the far right lane. They both fell. They were soon screaming at each other. Raghav pulled his motorcycle off the road and walked across to see if either of them was injured and needed medical attention. The traffic policeman on duty reached them at about the same time. The cyclist insisted on filing a case. The constable asked Raghav if he could come to the police station as a witness. The good citizen agreed readily. The constable's superior at the station house, a

Sub-Inspector, thoughtfully offered to take Raghav's statement first, so that he could be relieved. With his permission Raghav made a quick call home to explain his reaching late.

Name. Raghav Murthy.

Driver License? Produced, noted.

Address. As in Driver License? Yes, it will do. Father's name. S. Rangarajan Murthy.

Occupation. Software Engineer. Place of birth. Allahabad.

A pause. The Sub-Inspector looked up. He repeated the question. Place of birth? Raghav repeated his reply. Allahabad. And that is where it all started. A friendly banter at first, but soon it became serious business.

You mean Prayagraj? No, I mean Allahabad.

There is no Allahabad now. It is Prayagraj. But it says Allahabad in my Driving License.

That may be. But your place of birth is Prayagraj. No, sir, it is Allahabad.

Look, sir, let us not waste time on this. I have to enter it as Prayagraj. No, sir. You can't. I refuse to have my birth place shown as Prayagraj.

Another pause. They shifted gears. It got heated. The Sub-Inspector held on to the official line of the city's name, insinuating that those from outside the state of Uttar Pradesh had better learn to respect local culture. And local laws. Raghav reminded the Sub-Inspector that the highest court in the state was called Allahabad High Court. The Inspector thumped the table with his fist. Raghav tapped it with his knuckles and said those who swear by the name of Prayagraj do not know the glory of Allahabad.

That was it. The Sub-Inspector picked up the phone and dialled his superior in another office. Yes...yes...yes...all right... done! The Sub-Inspector issued the order that Raghav was to be kept in police custody until further notice. Before Raghav could ask, he barked out "...unruly behaviour, attacking a police official, disturbing the peace, hurting the sentiments of the community". He was escorted out by a havildar. Since Raghav did not have a criminal record, was well dressed, fair skinned and clean shaven, the custody was in an out-house at the back.. There was a pair of structures side by side. Each had two identical rooms with a bed, a desk and chair and a modha with arms. The wall on one side of the bed had open shelves made of concrete slabs. In the corner was a partitioned area with a floor lavatory, a tap, two galvanized iron buckets and an aluminium mug. The station compound wall on three sides of the out-house was high, with broken glass embedded on the top edge. A brick paved path led to the back verandah of the station. A constable was seated there all the time on a school master's wooden chair.

Custody. It is the favourite device of law enforcement to deal with troublemakers. Created for the District Magistrate in colonial times and cheerfully retained ever after, it needed no indictment and no proven guilt. It was a useful device to label a person guilty until proved innocent. It put the arrested person in a state of limbo with cleverly undefined duration and unknown outcome.

In their home in East Didsbury suburb the Raos received the news of Raghav's custody with amusement. Raghav! How on earth did good old Rags get himself in such a pickle? Amusement turned to amazement a week later, when the Murthys reported that he was still there. From a week to a month, and it was alarm.

Something had to be done. Rao senior called a schoolmate's colleague who had just retired from a respectable position in the Transport Ministry to understand what the long custody meant. And what might be done. The reply was not what could be called to the point. He was told instead how the price of tomatoes had gone through the roof in the last two weeks.

Raghu decided to make a trip to India. The family agreed immediately and set about the travel arrangements. He would stay with the Murthys, of course, and a plan of action would be drawn up after he got there.

The day after he landed he carried the tiffin carrier with Raghav's lunch to the station house. At first there was objection to his bringing the lunch, as he had not been registered as a family member. He had to get the Sub-Inspector's permission. Raghu took out a calling card and explained that he had come all the way to see his brother. Brother?

Cousin.

Same family?

Same clan, same jati.

The Sub-Inspector let him in, but asked him to stay back for a few minutes after the under-trial had eaten his lunch. He wanted to know about University options in England for his son.

The lunch remained untouched. They shared a bar of Swiss chocolate instead, one of a sizable bunch Raghu had picked up while in transit at Dubai airport. Two more bars were left behind for Raghav. They talked about many things, as they were meeting after three whole years. The constable in the verandah shouted out that it was time up. Raghu said he would bring lunch again the next day. They would then work on a plan to get Raghav out.

On his way out Raghu had a pleasant chat with the Sub-Inspector. He was asked if he was from Prayagraj too. Yes, of course, he was from Prayagraj. He was careful not to correct the officer. Ah, yes, Universities in the UK. Raghu offered to meet the Sub- Inspector's son for a chat. He would gauge his aptitudes and then recommend the right places. The officer gave him some parting advice. He suggested that Raghu should knock some sense into his cousin's head. If a young man living in England can be a sensible Bharatiya nagarik, why couldn't he?

⌘ ⌘ ⌘ ⌘ ⌘

"It is out of my hands". The Sub-Inspector was polite, even gracious, as he shared tea and biscuits with Raghu.

"In whose hands, then? Who has the authority?"

"You may laugh if I tell you I don't know, but that is the truth. It is up there somewhere".

"Can they keep anyone here this long? Is there not a rule about that?"

"Bhai saab, all rules are made up of – what do they call it – clauses. All clauses have sub-clauses...matlab, who knows what the real rule of law is...

"How do you decide?"

"I don't. I don't get into it. Not my job".

When asked who really decides, the Sub-Inspector said it was his boss in the Assistant Commissioner's office. An Inspector. So, the Inspector decides? Not really, as he has to put up the case for the Superintendent to put his signature and office stamp. So...would it be right to say that the Sub-Inspector can put up a case for Raghav's release, which would go to the Inspector in the Assistant Commissioner's office, who would put it up to the Superintendent? That was correct. The Assistant Commissioner would then approve it and countersign the case paper. Attached to the case paper would be a written apology by the under-trial, also stating that he had no malafide intentions.

The big question then was: how to get Raghav to write a letter of apology? It seemed an impossible proposition, knowing Raghav.

The Sub-Inspector admitted that he was willing to put up a recommendation, if only the man would cooperate...He had come to like Raghu. And Raghav was not such a bad fellow after all. It was just that he had not liked the way he defied the authority of the Sub-Inspector.

It looked like an important first gain. Raghu asked what the Sub-Inspector thought about a counselling session for his son.

"Arrey sahib, it was not for my son. I am stuck with two daughters. I was asking for the Inspector Sahib's son. In that big office. I know that nowadays his mind is all the time on a foreign education for his son. I thought – you know – if I can do him some service...I can talk to him about you."

In the next visit, Raghu left behind a folder with sheets of paper that had the names of eight Universities and Colleges in the UK. Under each of them was a list of courses for which there was low enrolment from India, although there were special offers.

There were also e-mail contacts given.

The counselling session was set up after one more tiffin carrier visit. The Inspector arranged a room for it in his own office building. The session was short, and hardly any counselling took place. The young man had a mind of his own. He wanted to get himself an MBA as quickly as possible. It was the best way to get ahead in life, he said. He wanted to know about one-year courses in the UK. One year of study, two years in a decent job there, and he would be set.

In the visit after that Raghu saw from a distance that the Sub-Inspector was standing at the arched entrance. He was beaming.

He extended his hand, a gesture Raghu was seeing for the first time. He led Raghu to his desk and ordered a constable to fetch two cups of special chai. They sat. A moment of silence, but he was still beaming. He then reached behind him and held up what looked like a basket of fruit. Like a magician concluding his signature act he swished aside the muslin cover on the basket. They were guavas. Large, cricket ball sized, just the right shade of green, bordering on pale cream.

"This is for you, sahib. From the Inspector. Best quality Safeda. Straight from Allahabad!"

About the Author

Vijay Padaki is a Theatre Educator based in Bangalore. He has worn many caps all his life with equal facility. Among them, he has been active in the theatre for over sixty years. He has been a management professional for over forty-five years.

Vijay joined Bangalore Little Theatre in 1960, the year of its inception, and later served the company in many capacities – as actor, director, trainer, writer, designer and administrator. In 2008, Bangalore Little Theatre Foundation was restructured as a Public Charitable Trust. It was done with the purpose of reinforcing the organisation's commitment to social development goals beyond performance. The Trust requested Vijay to provide the leadership to a newly-created Academy of Theatre Arts in its formative years.

Vijay has been responsible for institutionalizing several activities of BLT, such as the annual summer workshop for newcomers to the theatre (SPOT), from which has emerged a large number of the theatre personalities in Bangalore, the History of Ideas programme of biographical plays, the Courtyard Theatre programme, and the Children's Theatre programme, which includes the annual flagship children's play as a partnership production to support a charity. Vijay conceived and initiated programmes for training trainers, training directors and promoting new writing for the stage. He has forged several international partnerships with BLT over the years. The Ministry of Culture invited Vijay to initiate a programme of Arts and Heritage Management in India.

Vijay has been a writer for many years. In addition to over 50 original plays published by Bangalore Little Theatre, he diversified into writing short stories. There are over 40 stories by him. He has done several readings of his stories in public spaces. Notion is publishing the first 36 stories in two volumes. Vijay believes that all writing is autobiographical. (To greater or lesser extent!) What that means is that life experiences have a way of creeping into everything we say. In other words, there is no need to deny it or be sorry about it. He says he has had the good fortune of exposures in life that had both breadth and depth. These included field experiences as part of his work in large development programmes in rural settings.

Vijay is a psychologist and behavioural scientist by training, and founder-director of a management resource centre with programmes of research, consulting and training in the areas of Organisation and Institutional Development. A good part of his work was devoted to the effectiveness of large development programmes. Among his earlier assignments he was a member of the founding faculty at Indian Institute of Management, Bangalore, the founder of a Centre for Management for the textile industry in Ahmedabad, and a Visiting Professor at Indian Institute of Science, Bangalore. He was a Senior Associate at the National Institute of Advanced Studies in its early years.

www.ingramcontent.com/pod-product-compliance
Lightning Source LLC
LaVergne TN
LVHW091307150826
845673LV00006B/1564

* 9 7 9 8 8 9 5 8 8 6 5 8 8 *